Seeing the figure dressed in black disappearing through her motel room window had shaken Megan badly. But the evidence he'd left behind was almost worse.

The killer was taunting her. Mocking her. Daring her to find him.

He'd turned the murder of a young girl into something personal.

When Luke pulled up in his squad car, she was relieved. "Are you all right, Megan?" he said. "Did he hurt you?"

She shook her head, breathing deep to control her emotions. "No, I'm not hurt." She turned and gestured to the interior of the motel room. "You'd better take a look, the intruder left evidence behind."

"So that leaves one question," Luke said slowly.

She tensed, knowing he'd come to the exact same theory she had.

"Why has Liza's killer targeted you?"

D0250103

Books by Laura Scott

Love Inspired Suspense

The Thanksgiving Target
Secret Agent Father
The Christmas Rescue
Lawman-in-Charge

LAURA SCOTT

grew up reading faith-based romance books by Grace Livingston Hill, but as much as she loved the stories, she longed for a bit more mystery and suspense. She is honored to write for the Love Inspired Suspense line, where a reader can find a heartwarming journey of faith amid the thrilling danger.

Laura lives with her husband of twenty-five years and has two children, a daughter and a son, who are both in college. She works as a critical-care nurse during the day at a large level-one trauma center in Milwaukee, Wisconsin, and spends her spare time writing romance.

Please visit Laura at www.laurascottbooks.com, as she loves to hear from her readers.

LAWMAN-
IN-CHARGE

Laura Scott

Love Inspired

Recycling programs
for this product may
not exist in your area.

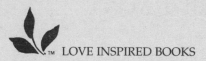 LOVE INSPIRED BOOKS

ISBN-13: 978-0-373-44446-5

LAWMAN-IN-CHARGE

www.LoveInspiredBooks.com

Printed in U.S.A.

The Lord is my light and my salvation—whom shall I fear? The Lord is the stronghold of my life—of whom should I be afraid?
—*Psalms* 27:1

This book is dedicated to my daughter, Nicole,
who has been reading my books
long before I sold my first manuscript.
Nicole, I love you and am very proud of you.

ONE

Megan O'Ryan kept a wary eye on the black sedan staying two cars behind her. She'd noticed the sedan the moment she'd hit the highway, and the driver had kept pace with her all the way into the small town of Crystal Lake.

A nagging itch settled between her shoulder blades. She'd felt the same sensation of being followed just two days ago. Was someone really tailing her?

With an abrupt move, she cranked the steering wheel to the right and pulled into the first vacant parking space on Main Street.

Moments later, the black car passed her by. Wrenching her neck to peer after it, she noticed the driver kept his head averted, but not before she saw the usual dark T-shirt and baseball cap. The tag number was nothing but a blur by the time she switched her attention from the driver to the license plate.

Megan climbed out of her car and stood for a moment, pretending to debate where she should go but really tracking the black car out of the corner of her eye as it pulled into the Gas N Go station located a few blocks north on Main Street.

No way could this be a coincidence. Not again. Not

after experiencing the same thing for the third time in the past week. The cars weren't always the same make or color, but the guy behind the wheel invariably wore dark clothing and a baseball cap tugged low over his eyes.

Megan stifled a surge of alarm as she turned toward Rose's Café. She wasn't hungry, but Rose's was always packed with people, especially in the summer with tourists aplenty, and she could at least get a cup of coffee while she tried to figure out why on earth anyone in Crystal Lake would want to follow her. Three months wasn't long enough to have made enemies. Especially considering she'd been holed up in her cabin most of the time, leaving only to go to work and back. She'd spoken to just a handful of people.

"Megan! Wait up!"

Katie? The young voice was so much like her sister's that she spun toward the sound, her heart hammering wildly in her chest. She blinked against the brightness of the sun to see a lithe young woman with long, silky blond hair walking toward her. Her heart stopped. She couldn't breathe. Hoarsely she called, "Katie? Is that you?"

"Teagan, wait up. Didn't you hear me?" The blond-haired girl changed directions, moving toward another girl, this one a petite redhead. The blonde caught up and gave the red-haired girl's shoulder a playful shove. "There's no rush. It's not like the guys are going to leave without us."

Not Katie. Her vision blurred as the loss hit with the force of a tsunami, sucking every bit of oxygen from her lungs. Katie hadn't been calling her name because Katie was gone.

Megan blinked, forcing her vision to clear, and watched the girls cross the street heading toward a group of boys who stood waiting on the grassy bank of Crystal Lake. She focused on a scowling boy who held himself aloof, dressed head to toe in black with long dark hair that could have used a comb. He looked like trouble with a capital *T.* Someone she was tempted to warn the young girls about. Except he wasn't her problem.

Blindly, she turned her attention back toward Rose's Café, her stomach tight with nausea, as if she'd been sucker punched.

Katie wouldn't be heading off to her sophomore year at college in the fall, or hanging around with undesirable boys. Katie was dead.

Murdered.

Logically, she knew her younger sister was gone. Yet in that one brief moment when she'd imagined she'd heard Katie calling her name, she'd wanted so badly to believe Katie's death was nothing more than a horrible nightmare.

But it wasn't. Katie was gone.

Her church pastor tried to tell her Katie was in a much better place, but she didn't buy that theory. The real question was why hadn't God stopped her sweet sister from being murdered? Why hadn't he taken her, instead?

Desperately trying to get a grip on her rioting emotions, she paused outside Rose's Café and glanced once again toward the Gas N Go station, where the black car had pulled in. There was no sign of the vehicle now. With a frown, she scanned the entire area, including the various businesses.

The black sedan had disappeared.

Or she'd imagined the whole thing, just like she'd imagined she'd heard Katie.

Exhausted and shaken, Megan slumped against the building, putting a hand to her throbbing head, and swallowed hard against another wave of nausea. "No. No way. I absolutely refuse to be crazy."

"You refuse, huh?" A tall man stepped forward, blocking her view of the sun. He stood with his arms crossed over his uniformed chest, looking down at her with an arched brow. "So how's that working for you?"

She grimaced, realizing she'd spoken out loud. Wasn't it true that insane people didn't believe they were crazy? Shaking off the bitter fear that plagued her, Megan straightened and belatedly noticed the crisp tan uniform along with the shiny badge pinned to the stranger's chest.

A cop. Great. This was not what she needed in the middle of her nervous breakdown. She strove for a light tone. "So far, it's working fine, thanks. Excuse me." She ducked past him, seeking refuge in Rose's Café.

She slid onto the only vacant stool at the counter, figuring she wouldn't be there long. The main reason she'd come at all was to get a good look at the guy driving the black car.

"What can I get for you, sweetie?" Josie, the middle-aged waitress, called all her customers "sweetie." Megan suspected Josie thought the term was easier than trying to remember so many names, especially in the height of the tourist season.

"A cup of coffee, please." She glanced back in time to see that the cop who'd followed her into the diner had joined another officer in one of the booths that lined the wall. She turned her attention back to Josie. She wasn't paranoid enough to think he'd followed her inside to keep an eye on her. Cops had to eat too. "Cream, no sugar."

"Is that all?" Josie arched an exasperated brow, propping a hand on her plump hip. "Sweetie, you picked the middle of the lunch rush to order a measly cup of coffee?"

Josie obviously wasn't pleased she'd taken a seat that an otherwise paying customer may have occupied. Since Megan wasn't sure her legs could hold her weight if she left, she tried to recall the menu. "Ah, I almost forgot. I'll take a grilled chicken sandwich too."

"Coming right up." Josie poured her coffee, pushed a container of cream at her, and then disappeared to give her order to the cook.

Megan sipped her coffee, trying not to notice how several of the locals stared at her with obvious suspicion. Since she'd taken over her aunt's property, a small cabin on the north shore of Crystal Lake, her status was barely one step above the tourists, but not by much. She'd moved here from Chicago, and people in the town of Crystal Lake, Wisconsin, seemed to carry a grudge against people from Illinois. She should be used to the sensation of being the unwelcome newcomer by now.

Crystal Lake wasn't a large town, but it was right in the middle of Hope County, which made it the hub of all county activities. The courthouse, the post office and the sheriff's department headquarters, to name a few. Her tiny log cabin was located ten miles outside of town on a very deserted road with an awesome view of the lake, nice and private, the way she preferred. So what if the general population of Crystal Lake considered her little more than a weird hermit? She didn't care.

Except when she was being followed.

She turned her head to peek at the pair of cops seated behind her. The taller of the two had impossibly broad shoulders and black hair kept military-short, which did nothing to soften his broad, rugged features. His square jaw was strong and firm, but his nose looked as if it may have been broken at one point. He had dark eyes and tanned skin that made his teeth look shockingly white when he smiled. He was definitely attractive, if you appreciated a tall man in uniform. Since the other cop was much older and shorter and had a slight paunch around his middle, she knew it was the taller man who'd overheard her talking to herself outside. With the sun glare in her eyes, she hadn't gotten a very good look at him.

What would he say if she went over to announce she thought she was being followed? Probably not much, since she'd also practically told him she was insane.

So how's that working for you?

Her cheeks burned and she ducked her head, deciding not to bother. There was no point when she hadn't even managed to get a simple license plate number. Once she had something solid to give them, she'd go to the authorities.

She took another sip of her coffee, reveling in the warmth of the mug despite the sunny day outside. A group from the back of the diner passed behind her on their way out. An elbow hit her hard in the back, causing her to spill her coffee down the front of her green blouse.

"'Scuse me," a gruff male voice muttered as the group left.

She clenched her teeth against a wave of annoyance

and dabbed at the stain. A moment later, Josie set her chicken sandwich in front of her.

"Need anything else, sweetie?" Josie asked, automatically refilling her coffee cup.

"No, thanks." She forced a smile and gave up on her blouse. Josie slapped her bill upside down next to her plate and sashayed away to attend to her other customers.

She didn't want to believe the jab to her back had been done on purpose, but she couldn't help but think so. Why she'd become a target, she had no idea. She wasn't hurting anyone. She wasn't even in town very often. She was either in her cabin or working her part-time and rather mundane job of processing DNA samples at the State Crime Lab in Madison.

Obviously, her level of paranoia was already several standard deviations from the mean. Picking at her chicken sandwich, she took only a few bites before pushing her plate away.

Post-traumatic stress disorder. Diagnosed by her psychologist after she'd testified against the serial killer who'd strangled Katie as his last victim. PTSD brought on from being the lead crime scene investigator in a series of murders that included her sister's. Every time she closed her eyes, she saw Katie's body lying sprawled on the asphalt with the bright orange hollow-braided rope wrapped around her neck.

The image would haunt her forever.

Her boss had forced her to step back from being the lead investigator, but she'd continued working on the case in the lab until she'd gathered enough evidence to nail the man who'd killed her sister. It was small consolation to know Paul Sherman was serving a life sentence in a high-security Illinois prison as a result of her work.

Megan sighed and scrubbed a hand over her eyes. She needed to get a grip. She wasn't being followed. The people of Crystal Lake weren't out to get her. And Katie, the sister she'd raised since their parents had died in a tragic car wreck, wasn't ever coming back.

She'd come to Crystal Lake to heal. To take a break. To find herself. Somehow, she needed to get over her loss. Now that the trial was over, she couldn't seem to find something to focus on. She tossed down some cash to cover her tab and Josie's tip before sliding off the stool and heading toward the door.

She really, really didn't want to believe she was going crazy.

Because if that were truly the case, sheer determination might not be enough to prevent the inevitable.

Lucas Torretti watched the petite woman, her shoulder-length red hair glinting brightly in the sun as she left the diner. She was pretty, in a wholesome girl-next-door kind of way. Must be the sprinkling of freckles across the bridge of her cute nose. And when she'd looked up at him, her bright eyes had been almost mesmerizing. He caught Frank's gaze and lifted his chin in her direction. "Do you know her? Or is she one of the summer tourists?"

Deputy Frank Rawson followed Megan's lean figure as she climbed back into her car. Out of the group of guys working for the sheriff's department, Frank was one of the few who didn't begrudge Luke's position as interim sheriff. Mainly because Frank had never wanted the job for himself. Frank was serving the last two years of his duty before taking a well-earned retirement. "Yeah, that's Megan O'Ryan. Moved into the old Dartmouth place. Lucille Dartmouth was her mother's sister."

Luke nodded, noting the make of her car, a white Pontiac Sunfire, as she pulled away from the curb. He memorized the tag number, thinking he might run her DMV record just for fun. "What's her story?"

Frank lifted a disbelieving brow. "What, have you been living under a rock? How could you not have heard about Megan O'Ryan? She's the infamous crime scene investigator that helped convict the St. Patrick's Strangler down in Chicago earlier this year. Her younger sister was the perp's last victim."

Ouch. That must have been rough. He vaguely remembered the story now. It had hit the national news because the crime scene analyst who'd helped put the pieces of the puzzle together had been removed from the case when they'd discovered her sister was the latest victim. But she'd continued working the case in the lab and had testified in court against her sister's killer.

No wonder she'd been talking herself out of going crazy.

"Which one is the old Dartmouth place?" he asked, curiosity winning out against his better judgment.

"Ten miles north as the crow flies, on the dead end of Barker Road." Frank flashed a knowing smirk. "Why? Thinking of dropping by for a neighborly visit?"

"Of course not," he responded, just a little too quickly. He tossed some money on the tabletop to cover their bill and stood. "Let's get back to work. I don't want to be late for my meeting with the mayor."

As they left, he thought again about Frank's directions

to Megan O'Ryan's cabin. He knew exactly where it was, even if he hadn't known the locals referred to it as the Dartmouth place. The cabin was isolated, being so far off the main highway. Was Megan O'Ryan afraid to be out there alone? Maybe he should make sure the deputies covered the cabin in their weekly rounds. Luckily, there wasn't a whole lot of crime in Crystal Lake.

He brought himself up short. Why this sudden surge of concern about Megan O'Ryan? She might be the most attractive woman he'd met in a long time, but he wasn't interested in a relationship. Not now, maybe not ever.

After his wife's death three years ago, his life had spiraled out of control. He'd hit the proverbial rock bottom, losing his job and almost losing custody of his son when he'd tried to drown his sorrows in alcohol. With the help of his pastor and God, he'd managed to pull himself together. But he'd soon realized Sam had gotten involved with a scary group of kids, so he'd packed up their things and moved them to Crystal Lake.

Working as a deputy on staff had been good enough for him, but he'd been given the job as interim sheriff three weeks ago when his boss had suffered a major heart attack and had subsequent quadruple-bypass surgery.

Despite the obvious resentment from his former peers, everything was going fine. Except for his relationship with his seventeen-year-old son, Sam. Over the past year and a half, things had gone from bad to worse. In fact, there were days he honestly believed his relationship with Sam would never recover.

Not that he intended to stop trying. He prayed every day for God to help guide them both.

Teenagers, he reminded himself. Teenagers were

tough on parents. If he survived Sam's teenage rebel-
lion, he could survive anything.

Luke finished his meeting with the mayor. He had
wanted to know if Luke would consider throwing his
hat into the running for the permanent job of sheriff
now that Dan Koenig, humbled from his close call with
death, had announced his retirement. Luke had promised to think about it, but in reality he knew life would
be more difficult than ever if he took that course of
action.

Besides, he'd never get elected sheriff. Not when most
of the guys in the department figured they had a better
chance of winning the election and barely tolerated his
presence in an interim role.

There was too much paperwork associated with being
the sheriff anyway. Back in his office he stared at the
mound that seemed to grow by the hour. He sighed.
Likely a few of the deputies would throw their name
into the race. They considered him an outsider because
he hadn't lived and worked for most of his life in Crystal Lake. The fact that he'd been a Milwaukee homicide
detective for ten years didn't seem to matter here, where
the good ole boys' club still played poker every Friday
night.

Luke wasn't much into playing cards.

Well after five o'clock, he headed home, knowing
the minute he hit the driveway that Sam wasn't there.
Sam was never home if he could help it, and most of the
time Luke had no idea where Sam was. Mayor Ganzer
would never have offered to support him in the election
for sheriff if he'd known Luke couldn't keep tabs on
his own kid.

Sam had promised to be home, but of course he wasn't. So much for trying to talk, even to ask how his son's day had been.

He looked for a note from Sam, and after finding no clues to his whereabouts, he pulled a cold bottle of water and a plate of leftovers from the fridge. Outside, he plopped into a wide plastic deck chair overlooking the lake. He closed his eyes and murmured a quick prayer before digging in, eating the spaghetti cold as he watched the activity on the water. Boats sped by, some towing skiers, others inner tubes, as locals and tourists made the most of the too-short Wisconsin summer.

Sam had a cell phone that Luke paid for. Not expecting much, he pushed the speed-dial connection for his son.

And almost fell of his chair when Sam answered. "Yeah?"

Nonplussed, he tried to think of something to say. Yelling at Sam for not being home wouldn't work. "Hey, how are you? I'm sorry I missed you."

"Fine."

He grimaced at the one-word answer but doggedly tried again. "What are you up to? Have big plans for tonight?"

"No."

Pulling every tooth out of his head without novocaine would be easier than carrying on a conversation with his son. "Oh yeah? So you're just hanging around? With anyone I know?"

A pause. "Doug. Look, I gotta go. See ya later." Sam hung up before he could remind his son that his curfew on Friday nights was twelve-thirty.

Luke snapped his phone shut, trying to look positively

on the one-sided conversation. His son had answered the phone. And he'd admitted he was hanging out with Doug. Maybe Sam was mellowing out a bit. Maybe Sam wasn't just biding his time until he was eighteen and finished with high school and could blow his father off for good.

Too bad he didn't really believe that.

The ache in his chest intensified, and he rubbed the area over his heart with his hand. Sam's resentment hurt. Luke was very afraid of losing his son, hardly able to find remnants of the good kid Sam had once been before Shelia died. Sam's lack of respect made him so angry. Yet Sam had only started getting in trouble after Luke lost control when cancer stole Shelia's life.

How long would his son pay for his own sins? He hoped and prayed it would not be for long.

Luke stared out over the water long after the hubbub of activity had died down. No-wake rules after dusk usually put an end to the fun. Or rather, he thought with a grimace, the fun took another form, like bonfires and parties.

Is that where Sam was now? Partying somewhere with the other high school kids? Drinking? Drugs? Sex? He had no idea what Sam was doing these days. He'd searched Sam's room for incriminating evidence but had yet to find anything. Sam was too smart to make it easy. Sam rarely invited anyone from high school over to the house, so he didn't really know his son's friends very well, except for Doug, who lived on the other side of the lake.

Sam hadn't exactly blended into the crowd when they'd moved in, and Luke wasn't sure how much had changed in the past year and a half.

He kept his police radio close at hand. He was always expected to be on call in case something happened. Luckily it almost never did. The worst thing he'd experienced was when Eric Landers got drunk and put a gun to his head. They didn't have access to a crime team, so he'd used his old homicide skills to make sure they weren't missing something. After examining the evidence, Dan Koenig and the ME had both ruled Eric's death a suicide. There had only been one other death in his short tenure here, a hunter who had been shot by accident when he'd stayed out past dusk. Tragic, but not a homicide. The two events had created a lot of stir amongst the locals, providing gossip fuel for weeks.

Luke was glad there weren't many crimes in Crystal Lake. It was one of the reasons he'd moved here. He'd hoped Sam would flourish in better surroundings. In a place where life was simple and there were fewer negative influences.

Please Lord, help guide Sam home. And help me to be patient with him. Help give me the strength and wisdom to know how to handle him. I'm asking You to watch over him, Lord. Amen.

Luke must have dozed, because his radio blaring next to him woke him up. "Sheriff? Sheriff? Do you read me?"

Night had fallen, and he reached for the radio, fumbling with the buttons. "Copy that. What's up, Tony?"

"Found a dead body floating in the lake."

Oh, boy. He had heard tourists who drank too much and fell out of their boats were not uncommon in the summer months in the area. And there was nothing worse than a floater. "Got an ID on the vic?"

"Yeah." There was a small silence. "You'd better get

out here, Sheriff. This girl is local and she didn't die by accident."

He shot to his feet, instantly wide awake, his gaze sharp in the moonlight. "What do you mean she didn't die by accident?"

"She was murdered." Tony's voice sounded strained. "Strangled with a towrope before being dumped in the water."

TWO

Megan had trouble falling asleep, and when she did she dreamed of Katie. Even though at some level Megan knew it was a dream, she still heard the sounds of a struggle as Katie fought her captor. Katie's muffled cry somehow pierced her consciousness and she awoke, her heart pounding as if she'd been the one attacked instead of her sister.

If only she could go back, to the night Katie had been murdered. Maybe if she'd gone with her sister to the pub, Katie would still be alive today. Katie had asked her to go along to Flannigan's, as she was planning to meet some new guy she'd met during her job in the college library, but Megan hadn't gone with her because she had to work early the next morning. So she sent Katie off by herself.

Only to be woken hours later to investigate a crime scene. Never in a million years had she expected to find Katie as the victim.

Megan splashed cold water on her face and then crawled back into bed and tried to fall back asleep. But as much as she needed rest, she kept hearing sounds outside. Wildlife, no doubt. After so many years in the city, the sounds of the animals took some getting used to.

A loud pounding on her door startled her so badly she almost fell out of bed. For a moment she wondered if she was dreaming again, but no, the pounding continued. Then it stopped. Her imagination? Or reality? She hated not being sure.

Her cell phone rang and she grabbed it from her bedside table, staring at it apprehensively, not recognizing the number. When was the last time anyone had called her? Her friend from Chicago, Shana Dawson, had probably called once or twice, but it had been so long ago she honestly couldn't remember. Hesitantly, she flipped open the phone. "Hello?"

"Megan? This is Sheriff Torretti. We need your help. I'm standing outside your door."

Relief that she hadn't imagined the pounding was quickly replaced by surprise that the sheriff had her cell number, and then replaced again by cold dread. She scrambled out of bed and grabbed her robe. "I'll be right there."

"Thank you."

Why would the sheriff need her help? She cinched the robe tightly around her waist and flipped on the porch light so she could see through the front window to verify that it was, indeed, the sheriff out there, before she unlatched the dead bolt on the door. When she opened it, she realized the man standing on her doorstep was the same one she'd met earlier that day outside of Rose's Cafe. She flushed. "Sheriff? What's going on?"

He hesitated a moment. "There's been a murder. I don't have access to a crime team and I really need your expertise."

Her first instinct was to refuse. She didn't go on-site to investigate crime scenes any more. She'd given up her career after Katie's death. These days, all she could manage was processing routine DNA samples. "Surely someone on your staff is qualified to gather evidence?"

He shook his head, his expression betraying his frustration. "In normal circumstances, yes, but we don't get many murders here. I've already called the Madison crime lab. They'll process our evidence of a serial killer, which they'd never believe considering we only have one victim. So as of right now, we're on our own."

She frowned, realizing he was right. Crime teams existed in big cities like Chicago, New York, and Los Angeles but not in small communities like Crystal Lake. Once she'd thrived on the details, the exactness of the work that helped piece a complex puzzle together. But since Katie's death, she'd lost her edge.

"I'm retired from CSI work," she protested weakly.

"Please?" She had the impression from the hard set to his jaw that he didn't beg very often, and the worried concern she glimpsed in his gaze tugged at her in a way she couldn't describe. "I'll take your rusty skills over nothing."

A murder. She shivered in the dark night. She'd always believed victims and their families deserved justice. Once she'd been at the top of her game, but not any longer. Yet could she honestly refuse to help?

No. She couldn't. Ignoring the dread curled in her stomach, she nodded. "Give me a few minutes to get dressed."

"Of course. Thank you."

She tried to smile as she closed the door, but her

hands were shaking. She took a deep breath and let it out slowly. She brushed her teeth and then quickly donned a pair of jeans, a long-sleeved T-shirt and her work boots before heading outside. Sheriff Torretti was waiting patiently beside his squad car.

"Where's the body?" she asked.

"On the south shore of the lake. You can follow me," he said as he climbed into the driver's seat.

She did as he requested, and all too soon, she followed him to a place where several cop cars, red and blue lights flashing, were parked in front of a path leading down to the lake. Carrying her camera and a flashlight, she climbed from the car.

"This way." Sheriff Torretti gestured toward the path.

She didn't walk down the path right away, but swept her high-powered flashlight over the scene to see if she could pick out any clues. She saw nothing more than a few bent and broken branches, indicating that someone, most likely the cops, had been down this way. Using her camera, she took several pictures, just in case.

She continued making her way down to the lake, acutely aware of the sheriff following behind her. Despite her initial embarrassment at being with him, she had to admit his presence helped her to feel safe.

When she reached the clearing, she stopped and once again scanned the area with the flashlight. "Have your deputies been down here?"

"Yes. Deputy Tony Markham pulled the victim out of the water because he didn't realize at first she'd been murdered."

"He found the victim?"

Luke nodded. "Yeah, apparently her mother called

when her daughter didn't come home at curfew, so he went looking for her. This path is used by the high school kids when they come down to the lake."

She didn't move, but swept her light around the wooded area, searching for clues. "Do you often have bodies washing ashore?"

His lips thinned. "No. Before I came there was a drunk tourist who fell off his boat and hit his head on the way into the water. But that was over two years ago. This is the first homicide in the eighteen months since I've been here."

Even one homicide in the small town of Crystal Lake seemed like too much. It took a minute for her to register what he'd said. He was relatively new to the area, just like she was. "Do you think the murder actually happened here?"

"I couldn't see anything to indicate the crime had taken place here. The lake is spring-fed, so there is a slight current running north to south. To be honest, this could have happened anywhere."

Not good news. It was always harder to find detailed evidence when a body has been moved. Even worse when the body was dumped in the water.

Interesting that this was the normal hangout place for the teens of Crystal Lake. If the crime had been committed elsewhere, had the killer chosen his spot on purpose, knowing the body would wash up here to be found quickly? Crystal Lake was several miles long and surrounded by woods. There had to be a zillion other places in the area to hide a body.

Fighting apprehension, she headed closer to the lake. A young female victim was lying on the bank, where the deputy had dragged her from the water. She flashed a light along the ground, seeing a mess of trampled footprints, more than just from the deputy, but she supposed if the kids were down here often, that wouldn't be unusual.

As she moved closer, the scene became surreal. The water changed to a blacktop parking lot at the corner of Flannigan's Irish pub. The young woman was lying at an awkward angle, the orange braided rope bright against her slim neck. Katie? No, it can't be. Katie? Katie!

"Are you all right?"

The deep voice beside her snapped her back to the present and she drew an uneven breath, trying to focus on the matter at hand. Her victim, the girl in the water, was blonde, just like Katie. Megan moved closer, focusing on her face, realizing with dread that she remembered the girl. "Oh, no," she whispered.

"What?" Luke Torretti followed beside her, careful not to disturb anything. "Do you know her?"

"Teagan," she murmured, remembering the scene outside the diner. "No, that isn't right, she called her friend Teagan. I don't know this girl's name."

"Liza Campbell, an eighteen-year-old high school senior." Sheriff Torretti's tone was grim. "When did you see her last?"

"This afternoon, just before I ran into you outside Rose's Café. She was heading down to the lake with a redhead named Teagan and they met up with a group of boys." Megan took another step and almost went to her knees. The rope wrapped around the girl's neck was badly faded, but in the light of her flashlight she would guess the original color had been red, pink or orange. Regardless of the color, it was polyurethane and braided.

Just like Katie's.

Luke saw Megan sway and reached out to grab her. Her arm was slim yet strong beneath his fingers. It was the second time she'd appeared about ready to faint. Maybe he shouldn't have asked her to come out here. "Are you sure you're all right?"

His question snapped her out of the reverie she'd fallen into. Her shoulders stiffened. "I'm fine." As if to prove it, she shrugged off his hand, lifted her camera and began taking pictures, pretending the brutal slaying of a young girl didn't bother her.

He stayed close, just in case, watching her work. Crime scene experts were usually not squeamish when it came to violent death, but having heard about Megan O'Ryan's history from Frank, he could understand what she was probably going through. Her younger sister had been strangled too. The similarities between the two crimes had to be difficult for her. Yet she approached the scene with cool professionalism, obviously stronger than her slim, petite frame looked.

She spent a lot of time looking around the area. She walked over to the fire ring not far off the lakeshore and bent to examine the ashes. "They're still warm," she murmured.

"I know."

Nodding, she stood and went back down to the young girl's body. "Rigor mortis has just set in, so I estimate the time of death is approximately within the past four hours."

He agreed with her assessment and knew the warm

ashes gave credence to her time frame. "I suppose the lake water washed away any evidence."

"Maybe, maybe not. There's still some mud embedded in the bottom of her running shoes. And I would recommend sending the faded rope around her neck to the lab. If the perp wasn't wearing gloves, there might be skin cells in the fibers of the rope. We could get lucky."

Luck wasn't his strong suit, but he nodded. He wasn't going to take any chances. Not with this. His first murder as interim sheriff.

Dawn was breaking over the horizon by the time the medical examiner left the scene, taking Liza's shrouded body with him.

Megan came up beside him. "Liza didn't die here. The dirt embedded in the bottom of her shoes has the consistency of clay. I can't see anything around here except sandy dirt and a bit of moss."

"So what do you recommend?" he asked.

She grimaced and shrugged. "It's a long shot, but we could do a broader search, to see if there's some other area around the lake where a scuffle might have taken place. Can you shut down access to the lake for a while?"

"We can shut down the public boat launch, but there are at least twenty-five dwellings surrounding the lake. I can send a few deputies out to ask everyone to stay off the lake, if you think it will help."

"I think it would help. We need to start as soon as we have more light."

"And what if she wasn't killed close to the lake?" Luke couldn't help but point out the obvious. "She could have been killed anywhere, there's natural forest for miles around. Don't you think your plan to search the entire lake is a bit extreme?"

"Extreme? Or inconvenient?" Her gaze bored into his. In the faint light he couldn't tell what color her eyes were, but for the first time tonight, there was a fiery determination shooting daggers at him. "If she was your daughter, don't you think a little inconvenience would be worth it to find her killer?"

Touché. As a cop he knew very well how family members of victims needed closure. She was right. He raised a hand in silent surrender. "Okay. I'll approve overtime for every single deputy to help us search." He'd better call the mayor too, because it was only a matter of time before both of their phones would be ringing from angry and worried citizens. Especially once they started questioning everyone, including the hordes of tourists.

"You're going to want to question Liza's friends, Teagan and the boys she went out to the lake with."

He swallowed the spark of annoyance. He had asked for her help, so there was no point in complaining when she gave it to him. "Yeah. I know." He could get the names of the boys from Teagan, no doubt, and Liza's best friend was exactly the place he intended to start.

Megan hesitated. "I realize I shouldn't make rash judgments, but there was one boy, lanky and tall, with long dark hair, dressed all in black, who seemed to be a loner, standing apart from the rest of the group."

His breath froze in his throat at her description. Long dark hair? Lanky and tall? Loner? Sam?

Was she really describing his son?

Oblivious to his internal turmoil, she continued, "He appeared angry, a deep scowl on his face. I remember thinking he looked like trouble. Maybe his anger got the better of him."

Angry accurately described Sam. Trouble did too. But even if his son had been at the lake last night, that didn't mean he'd had anything to do with Liza's death. As far as he knew, Sam hadn't been caught doing anything illegal.

Yet Sam hadn't been home earlier when he'd come in from work. And he'd claimed he was hanging out with Doug. Luke thought back to when he'd gotten the call about finding Liza. He'd torn out of the house, heading straight to the crime scene without checking Sam's room.

But now that he thought about it, Sam's large, rusted, black four-wheel-drive Chevy truck hadn't been in the driveway when he left. His gut clenched again. What time had the call come in? Quarter after two in the morning?

He told himself to relax, that Sam often didn't come home by his curfew. He'd verify where Sam had spent the night, and it was highly likely Sam had a decent alibi.

Sam claimed to hate Luke for moving them to this small, podunk town, as he described it. But Sam wasn't a bad kid. He may have gotten into a few fights, but always with other boys, never taking his anger out on a girl. Sam was quiet, not doing well in school, but that was normal teenage stuff. No, there was no reason for him to worry about Sam, not over something like this.

Not cold, premeditated murder.

"Thanks for the information," he said, when he belatedly realized Megan was waiting for his response. "Don't worry, we'll check into every possibility."

"I'm sure you will." Megan looked slightly embarrassed, as if realizing she was ordering him around. She gave him a strained smile before turning toward her car. "We'll need decent light, so I'll meet you at the diner in three hours to start the search."

"I'll have everyone ready to go by then," he agreed.

He watched her drive off. He didn't leave right away. First he made his phone calls, ordering the deputies to report to work and then leaving a message for the mayor. Once those two most important tasks were finished, he debated between going home and going straight to the office.

After a short internal argument, he headed home. He told himself the main reason was to change clothes, knowing that this was going to be a long day with potential media exposure. As the interim sheriff, he was expected to be in uniform at all times.

But his heart squeezed in his chest when he pulled into the driveway.

Sam's truck still wasn't there.

Luke strode into the house, straight down the hall into Sam's room. The bed wasn't made, but then again, it rarely was. He stood in the center of the room, looking for some sign, anything to tell him that Sam had been there at least at some point during the night.

Dark clothing was scattered all over the floor, but he couldn't tell if any of the garments had been recently worn and discarded. His son's entire wardrobe consisted of black T-shirts and black jeans. Luke had taken some dirty dishes out of Sam's room the day before, and there were no recently used plates or glasses lying about to indicate he'd come back at some point during the night.

Nothing at all to indicate Sam had been here. Luke swallowed hard.

Did that mean he didn't have an alibi? That maybe his son had been with the dead girl? Sam did seem to be angry, but surely not angry enough to take someone's life.

He desperately needed to find Sam, to question him before one of his deputies did.

THREE

Megan decided to eat breakfast at Rose's Café before meeting Luke and the rest of his deputies to begin the search. She wasn't really hungry, but her brain needed nourishment in order to remain sharp enough to find any clues as to where Liza might have been killed.

The similarities between Liza's death and the victims of the St. Patrick's Strangler, as the press had dubbed Paul Sherman, bothered her. She wanted to talk to the sheriff about her suspicions, but he hadn't been at the office when she'd stopped by on her way back to the café.

Josie was behind the counter again. Megan ordered an omelet for breakfast and then asked Josie if she'd seen the sheriff recently.

"He's out back, sweetie, talking to his son."

"His son?" She couldn't hide her shock. "He's married?"

"Widowed." Josie grinned, enjoying the gossip. "His boy runs a little wild, though, if you know what I mean."

Widowed. Why the tragic news made her feel a mixture of sadness and relief she had no idea. Megan slid off her stool and walked outside, circling the corner of the diner. She stopped abruptly, remaining semi-hidden behind the Dumpster, when she caught a glimpse of Sheriff Luke Torretti facing down his son.

"How long have you been drinking?" Luke asked in a low furious voice.

"What do you care?" The boy was the same one she'd noticed the day before, the tall, lanky kid with the long, dark tangled hair, only today his hair was pulled back in a stubby ponytail, partially hidden by the paper hat the boy wore. Dressed in scruffy jeans and a long apron tied around his narrow waist, he looked to be the café dishwasher.

She should leave, go back inside rather than stand here eavesdropping, but investigative instincts she'd thought long dead came to life, preventing her from leaving.

"You're right, Sam. Why should I care? So what if you go to jail? So what if you're convicted of strangling Liza Campbell? Why would I care about what happens to you, when you don't?"

The boy, Sam, blanched, and Megan thought he looked ready to throw up. Maybe it was a hangover from the drinking Luke mentioned or the blunt description of Liza's death. "Doug will vouch for me. I slept on the floor of his bedroom."

"And what time was that exactly?" Luke didn't give his son an inch. "Because from what I'm hearing, you were the last one to see her alive, and your only alibi during the time of Liza's murder is your best friend Doug."

"That's really great, Dad. Thanks a lot." The familiar sneer was back on Sam's face. "It's really nice to know my own father suspects me of killing some stupid chick."

"Stupid chick?" Luke's voice had gone dangerously soft. "Is that what you think of her? What's the matter, Sam? Did she turn you down when you asked her out? Did she look down her nose at you? Make you mad? Did you have a fight? Tell me what happened between the two of you. If you come clean and tell me everything now, it will be better for you in the long run."

Something in Luke's tone must have warned Sam not to push it. Instead of hiding behind sarcasm, he responded to his father's questions. "I didn't fight with her. I never asked her out. She wouldn't have gone with me anyway, she's still hung up on Sean Mathews."

"Is Sean her boyfriend? Was he with you guys last night?"

Sam shook his head. "No, Sean left two weeks ago to join the army. He's in basic training down in Kentucky somewhere. Liza was mad he broke up with her."

"So your story is that Zach, Doug, Teagan and Patrice left first, but you stayed behind a little while longer to talk with Liza. At midnight, you left Liza and went back to Doug's house. There were six of you at the bonfire and you split a case of beer. After you and Doug went to his house, you sat around and finished off a bottle of Jack Daniels while playing video games."

"Yeah." Sam stared down at his feet for a long minute. "That's what happened. Liza was fine when I left."

"You let her go home alone?" Luke pressed.

Sam flushed with guilt. "I offered to take her home, but she said she'd be fine. She gave me the impression she wasn't going straight home. I figured she might be meeting someone else. None of my business what she does in her free time."

There was a long pause, as Luke digested that information. "How often do you drink?" Luke finally asked.

"Not that often." The way Sam avoided his father's gaze made Megan believe he wasn't being honest.

"And you didn't bother to come home last night, or to call to let me know you were planning to spend the night at Doug's." Luke's sarcastic tone made her wince in sympathy for Sam, although it sounded as if the kid deserved it. She would have been just as upset if Katie had pulled such a stunt. "And where were Doug's parents while you were drinking?"

"His parents are divorced. His mom works nights as a nurse at Hope County Hospital." Sam hunched his shoulders. "This is the first time we got drunk on hard liquor. Normally we just drink a few beers. Doug's mom is a nice lady, it's not her fault we were stupid."

"You're right about that," Luke agreed, his tone slightly bitter. "You and Doug were stupid. Really stupid. Drinking isn't going to help, Sam. Don't you realize by now that drinking is only going to make things worse?"

A heavy silence fell, and Megan wondered if she should choose that moment to interrupt. But then Luke dismissed his son. "Get back to work. One of the deputies might need to ask you some questions later."

Sam looked as if he wanted to say something more, but he clamped his mouth shut and spun on his heel, walking back into the back door of the café. Luke turned and saw her, his eyebrows pulling together in a small frown when he realized she'd heard at least a portion of his conversation with his son. "You were right," he said with a grimace. "He is trouble."

She bit her lip, a twinge of sympathy making her regret her rash statement. She took several steps, closing the gap between them. "I'm sorry," she said in a low tone. "I didn't realize he was your son."

Luke shrugged. "Not your fault." His shoulders drooped, as if the interaction with his son had worn him out. He reached up and rubbed the back of his neck. "Was there something you wanted?"

"Yes." She had to pull her thoughts together, having been distracted by the emotionally charged interaction between father and son. "It's about the murder."

He lifted a brow. "Yeah?"

She let out a breath in a soft sigh. "I'm sure you noticed the similarity between this most recent murder and the series of strangulations I worked on last year. Specifically, the choice of murder weapon."

"The hollow-braided rope?" Luke asked.

She nodded. The rope disturbed her. Granted, the previous victims were all killed with a bright orange, brand-new rope, but still, could this really be a coincidence?

"You think we have some sort of copycat killer?" Luke guessed.

"It's a possibility." Megan glanced around, making sure they were alone. "Polyurethane hollow-braided rope is very common, especially here on a lake where there are lots of boats. And they come in all different colors. Why did the killer pick one that looks like it might be faded orange?"

"I don't know." Luke was frowning again. "We're going to verify the color, since it was hard to tell for sure if it had been orange or not. But regardless, the details of the St. Patrick's Strangler aren't a secret. Not anymore."

"I know." She shivered, in spite of the warmth of the sun. "Paul Sherman is serving a life sentence in prison for killing my sister, and even though he denied killing any of them, he doesn't have a chance at parole. I'm sure you would have heard about it if he'd have escaped from prison, right?"

"Yes," he assured her. "I already checked. He's still in custody."

She felt light-headed with relief. "Okay, so if Paul Sherman is in prison, the person who killed Liza might have tried to imitate parts of his crimes."

"But not all the details," Luke argued. "He tossed Liza's body into the lake. From what I remember, none of the other girls had been dumped in the water."

"True. Sherman stalked his victims at Irish pubs and killed them after closing. All three of them were blonde, all three were strangled with a brand-new orange poly-urethane rope, and their bodies were left within a stone's throw of whichever Irish pub he met them at."

There was a small pause. "I'm sorry about your sister."

Her throat swelled with guilt and sorrow and she couldn't speak, but she nodded. Seeing Katie's dead body had been the worst thing she'd ever gone through, worse than losing their parents to a car crash four years earlier. The only good thing was that she'd helped find evidence linking Paul Sherman to the murder of her sister. Katie had clawed at his hands, not knocked out by the drug concoction he'd put in her drink. She'd found skin cells buried beneath her sister's fingernails. The

DNA evidence had helped convict him. He claimed to be innocent, but the jury had found him guilty of all three murders.

"I'll have to review the trial transcripts," Luke said in a low tone. "See if there are other similarities."

"Good idea." She was grateful he wasn't ignoring her concerns. She couldn't say why the faded hollow-braided rope bothered her so much. She couldn't help wondering if the killer's choice was significant.

Unless she was simply becoming obsessed, because of Katie. For all she knew, this was simply a crime of opportunity and nothing more.

If the killer was a copycat murderer, why not match all the details? Brand-new bright orange hollow-braided rope instead of old, faded stuff? Leaving the body at the crime scene?

Maybe she was making more out of the similarities than she should be.

"When do you want to start searching?" Luke asked.

She remembered the omelet she'd ordered. "Soon. I have food waiting for me inside. Give me twenty minutes."

"All right, I'll have my deputies waiting at the south shore where we found Liza's body. You can let us know how to proceed from there."

The way he deferred to her expertise impressed her. The sheriff was obviously a man who didn't mind getting help when he needed it. And as far as she was concerned, they'd need all the help they could get to catch this guy. "Sounds good."

He nodded and walked away, so she headed back inside the café.

Her food was cold, but she ate it anyway. She couldn't help thinking about Luke. And his son, Sam. Despite what she'd overheard, especially the part where Sam had been the last one to see the victim alive, she really didn't want to believe Sam was guilty of murdering Liza. As angry as the teen was, it was difficult to imagine him capable of murder.

Because he was the sheriff's son? Maybe. Because she wanted to believe the best of him? Probably. Although she was forced to admit Sam seemed just as aloof and alone as his father.

Not that the ruggedly attractive sheriff was any of her concern. When her fiancé, Jake, had dumped her after Katie's death, right when she'd needed him the most, she'd decided she was better off without men, including tall, dark, handsome cops. Her main concern right now was to find the spot where Liza had been murdered.

There was always a clue. Sometimes the clues didn't mean much by themselves, but in the end, the truth prevailed.

When she finished breakfast, Megan drove back to the south shore of the lake where Liza's body had been found. True to his word, the sheriff had well over a dozen men waiting.

Since they all looked at her, she fell into the role of leading the investigation.

"We'll split into groups of two," she announced. "That way we can take our time and really search for clues. I'd rather have you pick up every small clue that might be evidence than overlook something important."

Luke stepped up. "The victim was wearing a light blue tank top and denim cutoff shorts. She had long blond hair. A hard, clay-like substance was found embedded in the heel of her right shoe."

The group of deputies and retired deputies, mostly men except for two younger women, all nodded solemnly, filing away the bits of potential evidence, and then split up as directed.

She and Luke split up. She paired herself with one of the deputies, named Adam. They started at the shore and then fanned out in opposite directions. The work was slow. She moved at a snail's pace for fear of rushing over some minute piece of evidence. She found a long dark hair that reminded her of Luke's son, Sam. She bagged it for evidence and marked the spot. She also found a thread, possibly a piece of denim, and followed the same routine. There were several empty bottles of Point beer, evidence of the partying she'd heard Sam talk about. She placed her third marker there before continuing her search.

Mostly, she found a lot of nothing. But she didn't give up. Sheer determination kept her moving forward.

Her radio crackled a few hours later and she heard a female voice. "We found something! A large area where an obvious altercation took place. A small footprint that looks like it may belong to the victim and a piece of blue thread."

Exhilaration filled her lungs. They must have found the scene of the crime. She swiped a sweaty arm over her brow and pressed the button on her radio. "Excellent work. Where are you?"

"We're on the north shore. The suspected crime scene is about fifty feet from a tiny log cabin. There's a red canoe tied to the dock on the lake."

Megan's radio slipped from her fingers, hitting the

ground at her feet with a soft thud. Tiny log cabin with a red canoe. Her house. A wave of nausea dropped her to her knees.

Liza Campbell had been murdered fifty feet from her back door.

Luke stood beside Megan, both of them watching as the deputies took several photographs and bagged the evidence from the area where they believed Liza had died.

A stone's throw from Megan's backyard.

He slid a glance at Megan, who stared straight ahead, as if completely lost in her thoughts. She was pale, deep circles cutting a groove beneath her eyes. With her arms crossed over her chest, she seemed to be holding herself upright. He suspected a stiff breeze would have blown her over.

"You didn't hear anything?" Luke finally asked, breaking the heavy silence. She didn't move, didn't acknowledge in any way that she'd heard him, so he repeated the question. "Megan? You didn't hear anything last night?"

She shook her head slowly, turning to face him. "Not really. I had a nightmare, about Katie's murder, and in my dream, Katie cried out in pain, fought her attacker—" Her voice broke, and she drew a deep, steadying breath. "Maybe it was Liza I heard and not Katie. I wish I knew for sure."

"Do you have a time estimate?" He hated asking, hated the need to push her to relive the horror, but he suspected she had heard Liza, and it was her subconscious that put Katie in the role of the victim.

Her sister's death obviously still haunted her.

He understood, considering he had a few problems of his own. Although he was much better now that he'd found his way back to God. He found himself wondering if Megan had the same spiritual support.

She rubbed a hand over her eyes. "Twelve-thirty, when I woke up and looked at the clock. But it seemed as if I heard Katie much earlier than that. Her struggle with the attacker lasted forever."

He wasn't so sure. Dreams had a way of seeming like hours, when in reality they were only a few minutes. Twelve-thirty was probably right on. If Sam was telling the truth, he'd left Liza about midnight. Liza must have been accosted as she headed for home.

But that didn't explain how the killer had gotten Liza so quickly from the south shore, where the kids were partying, to the north shore, where the crime actually occurred. Or why. Why had he chosen this place, so close to Megan's house, to kill Liza? Why hadn't he picked something more remote? There was plenty of deserted lakeshore around.

Unless the killer hadn't seen the house in the dark? Was he a stranger to the area? Would be a bit of a coincidence if the killer tossed the body in the water where it just happened to drift from the north shore to the south shore, right where the kids had partied around the bonfire.

Luke frowned. In his line of work, he didn't believe in coincidences.

Had the killer watched them during the bonfire? Struck out at Liza at just the right time? He could imagine how that might have played out.

The guy hadn't picked Liza by accident. No, he believed she'd been chosen on purpose. Either because this was personal, against her in particular, or because her long blond hair fit his profile. Especially if he was indeed a copycat killer.

He stood by Megan, silently supporting her, as his deputies finished with the crime scene.

The hour was close to dinnertime and he wanted to talk to Sam, yet hesitated to leave Megan alone. "Are you going to be all right here?"

"Sure." The response came automatically.

"Megan." He couldn't leave her, not like this. He lightly touched her arm, feeling strangely concerned about her. "Is there somewhere else you can go? I don't like you being here alone in this remote cabin fifty feet from where a murderer killed a young girl."

She shivered beneath his touch, and he knew she was struggling to remain calm. "I'll be fine. I don't know anyone in the area to stay with."

It was on the tip of his tongue to offer his place, but he knew that would be inappropriate. Besides, he still needed to talk to Sam, and he wouldn't welcome an audience during his lousy attempt at being a father. Bad enough she'd heard him lose his temper this morning.

"How about the motel?" he suggested instead. "It's located in the middle of town. Plenty of people will be nearby if anything happens. I can have the deputies cruise by on a regular basis." The more he thought about the idea, the more he liked it. "Please? I'd feel better if you were someplace safe."

"All right," she finally agreed. And the flash of relief in her gaze proved she was as loath to stay in this remote cabin as he was to leave her there. "I'll go to the motel, at least for tonight."

"Good." He couldn't hide his satisfaction. "Thank you."

"I—uh—need to pack an overnight bag." She headed toward her front door. On the steps she paused, and then turned back to him. "Sheriff?"

"Luke," he interjected quickly. "Call me Luke."

She gave an almost imperceptible nod, her gaze serious. "Luke. The way Liza was killed right next to my cabin—do you think it's possible the killer has specifically targeted me?"

FOUR

The dark apprehension shadowing her green eyes made him anxious to reassure her. "Megan, if he's a copy-cat killer, he would stick to the same M.O. of targeting young blonde girls," he gently pointed out. He didn't like how close Megan's cabin was to the crime scene, but he also didn't want to make more out of it than the situation warranted. "And we don't even know for sure that he is a copycat killer. Liza recently broke up with her boy-friend. Supposedly Sean Mathews is in Kentucky, but so far, we haven't been able to verify his whereabouts."

She worried her lower lip, not looking convinced.

"You know as well as I do that murders are commit-ted, more often than not, by people close to the victim rather than by random strangers."

"Yeah, I know the statistics," Megan said slowly. "But the braided rope really bothers me."

Luke couldn't deny the resemblance to the St. Pat-rick's Strangler bothered him, too. "You're right, but considering the number of boats around here, it could also mean nothing. In a crime of opportunity, the boat tie may have been the most convenient, logical choice. It was old and faded, after all, not brand-new like the ones used by Sherman. Makes me think this murder might not have been premeditated. Regardless, it would be stupid to lock ourselves into one specific theory. As far as I'm concerned, all possibilities are wide open."

There was a long pause as Megan seemed to consider his words. Then she straightened her spine, tilted her chin and immediately looked less like a victim and more like an investigator. "Smart thinking, especially this early in the investigation." The corner of her mouth kicked up in a small smile. "Give me a few minutes, and I'll be right back."

He didn't mind waiting, the various theories swirling around in his mind. He wasn't just reassuring her, although he wouldn't deny it was an added benefit. He seriously planned to keep all possibilities open. Especially since they hadn't found Sean, Liza's boyfriend, yet.

Especially since he was the interim sheriff and everyone would be watching and waiting for him to screw things up.

When Megan came back outside, he followed her little white Sunfire all the way into town until she was safely settled into her motel room. He'd requested one in the front, right in the center of the string of rooms.

"Thanks, Luke," Megan murmured when she slid her key into the door of room number four.

He stuck his hands into his pockets, since he was tempted to reach out and touch her. "You're welcome. See you in the morning." Ignoring the twinge of regret, he walked back out to his squad car. Turning around, he headed in the opposite direction from town, toward home.

He had to stop thinking about Megan and concentrate on his son. Sam was the most important thing in his life. As much as he dreaded the confrontation, he and Sam needed to have a serious heart-to-heart conversation about his underage drinking.

The discussion with Sam didn't go well. Partially because he was the one who did all the talking, while Sam sat sullen-faced and full of resentment. He lectured Sam on the perils of drinking, but Sam continued to deny he had a problem, claiming he normally only drank a couple of beers. Of course, even a couple of beers were illegal. But when Luke had finished his lecture, he was convinced his plea had fallen on deaf ears.

After Sam disappeared into his room, he pocketed Sam's truck key as punishment and went outside for a few minutes to clear his head.

Tipping his head back, he gazed up at the stars.

Please Lord, guide me in the best way to approach Sam. I don't believe he's guilty of anything more than being foolish in his desire to fit in with the other kids. Please show him the way. And keep my son in Your care. Amen.

Megan stared at the television screen in her motel room, her brain unable to stay focused on the lame sitcom. She should be exhausted after being awoken in the middle of the night, but she wasn't. The hour was still early, and the four walls of her room were already making her feel boxed in. She debated the wisdom of going to Rose's Café for something to eat. The diner wasn't far, just two blocks down the center of Main Street.

She rubbed her hands over her arms, trying to shake the deep uneasiness that had plagued her since the moment she'd gotten that call over the radio about finding the location of Liza's murder.

Fifty feet from her cabin.

She barely suppressed a shiver. Especially knowing she must have subconsciously heard the attack, dredging up memories of Katie. But there was no reason to panic. The sheriff was right, there were many theories to consider, not least of which pegged Liza's former boyfriend as the possible assailant.

Steeling her resolve to treat this like she would any other case, she picked up her purse and her cell phone and left the hotel room, making sure the door was securely locked behind her.

She shouldn't have been surprised to discover the center of town was busy, especially on a Saturday night. The streets were teeming with tourists who'd converged upon their small lake town. The lights were bright, making her feel safe as she walked to Rose's Café, hanging on to her purse the way she'd learned in downtown Chicago as she slid through groups of strangers.

Josie wasn't behind the counter. A pretty young blonde was working back there instead, and she couldn't help feeling a pang of disappointment. Josie might be a gossip, but at least she was a friendly face.

There was one last seat at the very farthest end of the café counter, so she slid into it gratefully. She ordered a veggie lasagna and sipped her water as she waited for her meal.

When a cell phone rang, it took her a minute to realize it was hers. Twice in one day. Had to be a record.

She winced a little when she saw Jake Feeney's name flash on her screen. Great. Her former fiancé. It was a sign of how lonely she felt that she answered the call rather than letting it go to voice mail.

"Hi, Jake," she greeted him. She was surprised he'd called; she hadn't spoken to him since before the trial.

"Megan! I'm so glad you picked up. Guess where I am?"

She frowned at his dramatic question, drawing circles in the water ring from her glass with her finger. "Where?"

"Crystal Lake. I decided to come up to see you."

Shocked, her jaw dropped as she tried to think of something to say. "Uh, wow, Jake, that's nice, but really you should have called first. I'm—uh—not at home." Which wasn't a lie. She wasn't at home. She was at Rose's Café.

"I know I should have called." Jake, as always, brushed aside her concern. From the background noise she could tell he was in a public area. "But come on, Megan, please? At least let me buy you a drink. I came all this way to see you."

Yeah, he'd come all this way, uninvited. She rolled her eyes, glad he couldn't see her. Really, his arrogance was amazing. She had no idea why she'd gone out with him, much less agreed to his spontaneous marriage proposal.

Spontaneous. Just like his showing up here unannounced. So typical of Jake. He was always one to give in to his impulses, without thinking things through. Amazing, considering he was a cop on the Chicago police force. But Jake was always reserved and serious on the job. Maybe that's why he liked to break loose during his off time.

"I'm in the middle of dinner," she said, as the cute blonde waitress slid a plate of food under her nose.

"After dinner, then. Meet me at Barry's Pub, it's right at the end of Main Street."

She shouldn't, but somehow the idea of going back to her minuscule motel room didn't appeal. "All right," she agreed, glancing at her watch. "Give me about thirty minutes."

"Great! See you then." He quickly hung up, as though afraid if she had a moment to think this through she'd change her mind.

She should change her mind, since getting back together with Jake wasn't even a remote possibility. She'd met Jake during one of her cases and he'd asked her out immediately. He'd broken things off just as abruptly, shortly after her sister's murder, claiming she was "obsessed."

Those dark days were the most difficult time in her life, and he'd simply walked away.

She'd missed his support, the ability to at least talk to him about her work, the clues she'd pieced together to bring Paul Sherman to justice once and for all. But once the trial was over and Sherman convicted, she'd reluctantly admitted she hadn't missed Jake, the man.

Being with Jake had been like riding a roller coaster. Exciting at times, but not something you wanted to do for the long term. Their ill-fated engagement wouldn't have lasted, even without the stress of the trial.

As she ate her veggie lasagna, she thought about how odd it was that Jake had showed up now, after all this time. She would have bet her entire bank account that he'd moved on to someone else without a second thought.

So why hadn't he?

Maybe her paranoia was rearing its ugly head again. She could be exaggerating the reason for his presence here. For all she knew, Jake had been in the area and in his usual impulsive way had decided to pop in to say hi.

Surely there was nothing wrong with having a soft drink with a friend?

She paid her tab, leaving a third of her meal on her plate, and then walked back outside. The pub was in the opposite direction from the motel, but not too far, so she set out at a brisk walk.

Inside the pub she paused, allowing her eyes to adjust to the dim lighting compared to the brightly lit streetlights outside. She saw Jake leaning against the bar, and when he caught her gaze and waved at her, she made her way toward him.

"Megan—" he caught her in a quick, hard hug "—I've missed you."

"Hi, Jake," she murmured, untangling from his embrace and wishing she could say the same. "What brings you to Crystal Lake?"

Instead of answering her question, he snagged the bartender's attention. "What do you want to drink?" he asked.

She tempered a flash of impatience. Jake knew she didn't drink alcohol. "Ginger ale, as usual."

He grinned and shrugged. "Hey, you made a totally radical change by packing up and moving to Nowhereville, Wisconsin, so I figured I should ask."

The bartender slid her soft drink before her and Jake waved a hand, indicating to put it on his tab.

"So how have you been, Megan?" he asked, leaning close. Too close.

She took a sip of her ginger ale, easing backward to provide more personal space between them and hiding a sense of discomfort. The moment she'd seen him, she'd known meeting Jake had been a mistake. "I really like it here, Jake," she said, avoiding his question. "Crystal Lake is a nice town, and living near the lake is peaceful." The locals hadn't welcomed her with open arms, but she loved being away from the city.

Away from the memories.

He snorted and took a healthy slug of his beer. She had to struggle to prevent herself from wrinkling her nose in distaste. "Yeah, if you like small towns." He flashed his most charming smile. "Look, Megan, I've been thinking about you a lot lately. I came up here to convince you to give me a second chance."

She almost choked on her soft drink. What? Why? "Ah, I don't know, Jake. I don't think I'm ready to be involved with anyone right now." The image of Luke's handsome face flashed in her mind, and she knew the statement wasn't exactly true. "I'm still figuring out how to get on with my life after losing Katie."

He stared at her, and for a moment something ugly flashed in his eyes, but in a heartbeat the strange look was gone. "Are you sure I can't convince you to change your mind?" he cajoled. "We had some good times, Megan. And I've changed. I swear I'm ready to settle down."

He was saying the right words, but there was something off about him. Every instinct in her body longed to get as far from Jake Feeney as possible. How had she actually agreed to marry this man? She must have had rocks for brains. "I'm sure," she said with more force than was necessary. "Sorry you came all this way for nothing, Jake."

He stared at her again for a long moment, making her irrationally nervous, until he let out a heavy sigh. "Hey, it wasn't for nothing, Red," he said, using the nickname she'd once thought was cute but now struck her as annoying. "At least I had the chance to plead my case. And I can be patient. If you're not seeing anyone else, I still have a chance."

She frowned again, thinking that it wasn't like Jake to plead his case to anyone. Maybe some woman had broken up with him and he'd figured he'd come see her, hoping she'd fall into his arms again.

Not.

"How's work going?" she asked, desperate to change the subject from their disastrous relationship.

He shrugged and glanced away. "Same old, same old."

There was another long pause, made even more uncomfortable because there wasn't anything more to say. Once work had been the primary thing they had in common, but not anymore. She downed the rest of her soft drink in a long gulp. "Thanks for the drink, Jake, but I really need to run."

"Hang on for a minute, I'll walk you out." Jake signaled the bartender for his tab. He signed off on the bill and tossed some bills on the bar for a tip before he shoved the receipt in his pocket.

He held the door open for her and then followed her outside. "If you change your mind, give me a call, Megan," he murmured, brushing a kiss on her cheek. "Take care of yourself, okay?"

"You too, Jake," she said, relieved when he stepped back. He pulled a ball cap out of his back pocket and put it on his head as he headed around the corner to the small parking lot behind the pub.

She turned to walk back up to her hotel, but then hesitated and spun around, going back to look for Jake. She scanned the parking lot but didn't see him. Was he still driving the yellow Camaro? If so, it wasn't in the lot. Maybe he'd bought a new car. But as she continued to watch the lot, nothing moved. Either he'd parked somewhere else, or he had already gone in the minutes before she'd come back. She waited for a few moments before she finally turned away, feeling foolish.

Really, she needed to get a grip. Just because Jake had slapped a ball cap on his sandy-brown hair didn't mean he was the guy who'd been following her for the past few days.

But the nagging possibility wouldn't leave her alone.

After a silent meal of frozen pizza with Sam, Luke went back to the office to work. For the first few hours he spent his time returning phone calls from concerned citizens and moving his piles of paperwork from one side of his desk to the other. He took the time to jot down all his theories so far, sheer busywork since they were already imbedded in his brain.

Because it was a weekend, they still hadn't heard back from the military bases he'd contacted to verify that Sean Mathews had truly joined up and was in basic training somewhere. Yet as much as he wanted to believe that possibility, he kept coming back to this being the work of a copycat killer.

At nine o'clock, he packed up the transcripts of

Paul Sherman's trial and headed home. He took a short detour, driving past the Crystal Lake Motel.

No sign of Megan; the windows of her room were dark. He sat in the parking lot for a few minutes, talking himself out of going inside to talk through the various theories. Finally, he shook his head at his own idiocy and told himself to forget about her.

For the first time in what seemed like forever, he was interested in a woman. But he wasn't free to pursue any kind of relationship. Not when he was failing miserably as a father to Sam.

All he could offer was friendship.

When he returned home, Sam's beat-up black truck was still in the driveway, so at least the kid hadn't hot-wired it. Luke knocked at Sam's bedroom door, listening for a moment, but didn't hear anything beyond his son's CD player belting out some heavy-metal noise disguised as music.

There was no response to his knock, so he opened the door a crack.

Sam glanced up from his computer, scowling. "What, don't you knock?"

"You didn't hear me," Luke said in an overly loud tone, hoping he'd made his point. "Just wanted you to know I'm home."

"Whatever." Sam kept his gaze focused on the computer screen, his fingers tapping out messages, no doubt to his friends, effectively shutting his father out.

For a moment, Luke was tempted to yank the computer keyboard right out from beneath his hands. He controlled the urge with an effort. Really, what did he expect? That Sam would just sit around and watch TV or play video games all day? He was seventeen, not seven.

Cutting a teenager off from his friends was a fate worse than death. So Luke called out, "Good night," before he stepped back and closed his son's bedroom door.

He sat at the kitchen table, reading through the transcripts from Sherman's trial, but when the words blurred on the page, he shoved them aside and stood.

Crossing over to the patio doors, he went outside to his favorite spot on the deck, overlooking the water.

The gently lapping water was mesmerizing. One thing about Crystal Lake, it was nice and quiet. When they'd first moved here, it had taken him a while to get used to the lack of noise. No traffic, no people, no sirens. Only the sounds of chirping crickets and belching bullfrogs echoing through the darkness. And the brightness of the stars overhead.

He'd grown to love it here. Too bad Sam hadn't found the transition quite as easy. Maybe if Sam would give up wearing nothing but black and cut his hair, maybe start listening to country music, he'd blend in with the crowd.

Yeah, and maybe he'd sprout wings and fly, too.

Luke scrubbed his face with his hands. At this point, all he could do was keep talking to Sam, even though his son hated every minute, and pray.

God would look after his son.

Just like the previous night, he was woken by his radio. "Sheriff? Sheriff, do you read me?"

He lifted a hand to his stiff neck. He really needed to stop falling asleep outdoors when he had a perfectly good bed inside. Pushing himself upright, he reached for his radio. "Yeah. What's up?"

"There was a break-in at the hotel. Some guy broke the lock on the window of the CSI's room and tried to get inside."

Megan's room? He shot upright. "Did you capture the assailant?"

"Negative. Unfortunately, sir, he got away. But the woman is asking for you."

He was already on his feet running toward his squad car parked in the driveway. "Tell her I'm on my way."

FIVE

Megan stood in the doorway of her motel room, her arms wrapped tightly around her waist as she struggled to maintain her composure. She'd changed from her nightgown to her jeans and long-sleeved T-shirt. The deputy who'd responded to the call was outside by the police car, since she'd refused to let him inside the room for fear he'd mess up the evidence.

The mostly empty beer bottle sitting on her bedside table mocked her. Seeing the figure dressed in black disappearing through her motel-room window had shaken her badly. But the evidence he'd left behind was almost worse.

Because now she knew for sure that the killer had targeted her, specifically. Liza's killer had been there. In her room. There was no doubt in her mind that the bottle of Point beer sitting on the bedside table had been left on purpose. And she strongly suspected that once they tested it, Liza's DNA would be found on the mouth of the bottle.

The killer was taunting her. Mocking her. Daring her to find him.

He'd turned the murder of a young girl into something personal.

The mere thought made her feel light-headed and sick to her stomach.

When Luke pulled up in his squad car, she was relieved. When he leaped out of the car and rushed toward her, his face full of concern, her fragile emotions broke through. She met him halfway, throwing herself shamelessly into his arms. They'd only known each other for a couple of days, but that didn't stop her from locking her arms around his waist and burying her face against his chest, deeply breathing in his reassuringly musky, male scent.

"Are you all right, Megan?" he murmured, resting his cheek against her hair and rubbing a hand on her back, soothingly. "Did he hurt you?"

She shook her head, breathing deep to control her emotions. "No, I'm not hurt." For several long minutes she reveled in the safe haven of his arms, reluctant to move, drawing sustenance from Luke's strength.

"Thank You, Lord," he whispered.

She stiffened in his embrace and pulled abruptly away. "Not exactly. God gave up on me a long time ago."

"What?" Luke seemed genuinely shocked by her comment.

But before he could say anything more, she turned and gestured to the interior of the motel room. "You'd better take a look. The intruder left evidence behind."

Luke frowned, and her attempt to distract him worked as he stepped past her.

"Evidence? Like what?"

She led the way back inside the tiny motel room. Luke sucked in a harsh breath when he saw the bottle of Point beer sitting on the bedside table. Her tone was dry. "Yeah, I can guarantee I didn't put that there."

"No, I'm sure you didn't." Luke stood there for several long seconds, surveying the room as she had, no doubt looking for the smallest detail. "Nothing else was taken or disturbed?"

"Nothing." Megan had done a quick inventory once the deputy had arrived.

"So why leave the bottle?" Luke asked in a low tone, almost as if he were talking to himself.

She suppressed a shiver. "I don't know, but I'm fairly certain we're going to find Liza's DNA on that bottle. He must have kept it as a souvenir of some sort."

Luke's expression turned grim. "We need to bag it and get it sent out to the crime lab in Madison."

"Yeah, that was my plan. But I didn't bring my gear with me." She shrugged apologetically. "I didn't imagine I'd need it."

"I have some gloves and bags in my trunk. How did he manage to get in without you hearing him?" Luke asked, swinging back toward her.

She flushed, feeling a little foolish and lifted her chin. "I didn't hear him because I picked up a pair of soft earplugs on the way home from dinner last night. With all the tourists walking up and down Main Street, the noise was incredible. I've gotten used to the peace and quiet of my cabin," she said, somewhat defensively. "Besides, if you look closely, you'll see he used a razor to cut out the screen. I left the window open for the cool breeze since the air conditioner smelled musty. It's a miracle I woke up in time to see him disappear through the window. I can't even tell you why I woke up when I did."

Luke nodded, his gaze thoughtful. "So that leaves one question," he said slowly.

She tensed, knowing he'd come to the exact same theory she had.

"Why has Liza's killer targeted you?"

Megan stood back as Luke bagged and tagged the Point beer bottle. When he finished, he came back toward her, taking a small notebook out of his breast pocket. "I need to take your statement, Megan."

She nodded, knowing the drill. For the second time in less than twenty-four hours, the killer had dragged her into his brutal crime. She sat down on the concrete curb and Luke lowered himself beside her.

"I decided to go down to Rose's Café for dinner," she began. "While I was there, a former boyfriend of mine called to say he was in town."

That news caused Luke to scowl. "Former boyfriend? What's his name?"

"Jacob Andrew Feeney," she supplied. "He's a Chicago cop."

"How long have you been seeing each other?" he asked.

"We're not seeing each other," she corrected, glancing up at him, her expression earnest. "Jake broke up with me right after Katie's murder. Claimed I was obsessed and he wanted to move on."

"Jerk," Luke muttered under his breath.

She flashed a crooked smile. "Yeah. Anyway, I haven't seen him or heard from him since the trial. So I was pretty surprised when he showed up here in Crystal Lake, uninvited." She couldn't understand the desperate need to make sure Luke understood she hadn't invited Jake to come up here.

There was a slight pause. "Did you meet with him?"

"We met at Barry's Pub and I had one ginger ale. He claimed he wanted to get back together with me, but I refused. I don't even know what I saw in him in the first place."

"So then what?" Luke asked.

She shrugged. "Nothing. We went our separate ways." She hesitated for a moment, then figured she'd tell him the rest. "But now is probably a good time to tell you that I think there might be someone following me."

"What?" Luke stared at her. "What do you mean, following you? Why didn't you say something sooner?"

"To be honest, I thought I was imagining things." She sighed. "I've been imagining a lot of things lately. I hear Katie calling my name. Twice I thought I saw her in a crowd of tourists. I have nightmares and flashbacks more often than I care to admit. I thought I was imagining the significance of the cars too, since they weren't the same make or model."

Luke briefly touched her arm, as if empathizing with her fear of going crazy. "Did you get any license plate numbers? Or a description of the driver?"

"No plate numbers unfortunately, but the driver is always some guy wearing a ball cap pulled low over his eyes, hiding his face." She felt better telling him everything. Maybe she wasn't going crazy after all.

But now she realized going crazy would be preferable to having a killer stalking her, targeting her.

Luke jotted a few notes. "You think it's possible this guy wearing the ball cap is our killer?"

Spoken bluntly out loud like that, the idea seemed

rather ridiculous. "I don't know," she admitted honestly. "I mean, logically, it doesn't really make sense, does it? Why would a killer follow me around for a week before picking out a young girl to strangle fifty feet from my cabin? And then follow me again to stash evidence from the crime in my motel room? For what purpose? To scare me? Theatrics? Because he wants to be caught?"

"Any or all of the above," Luke muttered.

She couldn't quite buy it. "Luke, if he has some sort of grudge against me, why not just come after me outright and be done with it?"

Luke's grim expression deepened. "I don't know. Maybe it's all a game to him. But this proves you need police protection, starting right now."

She nodded thankfully, hoping and praying police protection would be enough.

"Do you know if your ex-boyfriend is still in town?" Luke asked, closing his notebook.

"I have no idea," Megan admitted. But then suddenly, she glanced behind her at the string of motel rooms. What if Jake was indeed spending the night here at the same motel? The coincidence caused goose bumps to ripple up her arms.

"I'll check. Because I intend to have a serious chat with him."

"Do you really think Jake Feeney could be involved in this?" As much as Jake had annoyed her, she couldn't imagine him strangling an innocent young girl. "He's a Chicago cop," she protested.

Luke's dark gaze collided with hers, his mouth drawn into a thin, hard line. "I think anything is possible. And right now he's sitting close to the top of my suspect list."

* * *

Luke couldn't exactly explain why he was so irritated at how readily Megan defended that jerk of a former boyfriend. The guy walked out on her after her sister's murder. How cold and callous was that?

So why was she sticking up for him? And why had she agreed to meet him for a drink?

What Megan did in her personal time was none of his business. But he still didn't like it. Maybe because of the way she'd run into his arms. He'd been so glad to see her unharmed. The temptation to kiss her was overwhelming. Just thinking about Megan meeting up with her old boyfriend set his teeth on edge.

He tried to keep the foul mood off his face as he flashed his badge in the motel clerk's face. The elderly bald guy wasted no time telling him that Jake Feeney was indeed registered at the Crystal Lake Motel in room one.

Luke strode back outside and knocked on the door of room one. He didn't like disturbing the other guests at the motel, but he wasn't going to wait. He wanted to talk to Feeney now, not later that morning. When there was no immediate response, he knocked again, harder, and shouted through the door, "This is the police. Open up."

He heard a thump and a muttered curse before the door to the motel room opened a crack. "What do you want?" Feeney demanded, his expression haggard.

Luke flashed his sheriff's badge. "Open the door. I need to question you about a break-in."

For several seconds, he and Jake Feeney glared at each other. Then the other man let out a heavy sigh. "Give me a minute," he muttered before closing the door.

Luke waited impatiently, glancing back at his squad car where Megan sat hunched down in the passenger seat. Because of her personal relationship with the guy, he'd convinced her to allow him to question Feeney alone. Since the deputies were still dusting for prints in her old room, she'd agreed to wait for him in the car.

The door opened again and Feeney stood there, wearing a wrinkled T-shirt and jeans. A Chicago Cubs cap covered his head and his feet were bare. He crossed his arms over his chest. "What's the problem? There's been a break-in?"

"Yes." Luke was glad to notice that Jake Feeney was shorter and slighter in build than he was. A ridiculous thing to care about, but he couldn't help standing even straighter, looking down at the guy. "Tell me where you've been this evening."

Feeney scowled. "I was at Barry's Pub from about seven o'clock until closing. I came back here to my motel room at two in the morning and I've been here ever since."

Luke tried to peer past him. "Are you here alone?"

"Yes." Feeney's scowl went away and he smiled, turning on the charm. "Look, Sheriff. If you'll let me take out my wallet I can show you I'm a cop too. I didn't break in anywhere."

Luke nodded, mostly because he wanted to make note of the guy's badge number. When Feeney took out his wallet and opened it up he jotted down the number. "What brings you to Crystal Lake?"

The charm faded a bit. "I came to visit my former fiancée. I bought her a drink at Barry's Pub and we chatted for a while, but she left shortly after that."

Former fiancée? Luke narrowed his gaze. "You didn't leave together?" he pressed.

"We did, but then I decided to drown my sorrows at the pub, so I went back," Feeney admitted. "It's a short walk down Main Street."

Luke found his story a bit fishy. "You came all the way up here from Chicago to visit your old girlfriend?"

Something dark flashed in Jake's eyes. "Former fiancée," he corrected. "And yeah, I admit it was a bit of an impulse on my part. Things at work have been difficult, and I needed a few days off. I thought getting back together with Megan might help. I've missed her. My life was better when she was in it."

Interesting how Feeney wanted Megan to be there for him but he hadn't returned the favor when her sister was murdered. Selfish as well as being a jerk. "Your girlfriend's name is Megan O'Ryan?"

Feeney's eyebrows rose. "You know her?"

Luke didn't bother to respond. "Megan's room was vandalized at two-thirty this morning," he said. "Did you break in? Because you're carrying some sort of grudge after she refused to get back together with you?"

"Megan's room?" The flash of shock in Feeney's eyes seemed real. "I thought she lived in some remote cabin on the lake?"

His surprise seemed genuine, and he knew where Megan lived but hadn't known she was spending the night here in town at the motel. Could he be the man following her? Possibly. But even if he was, that fact alone didn't mean he was a murderer.

"You didn't answer my question," Luke said stubhornly. "Are you mad at her? Do you have some sort of grudge against her?"

Feeney crossed his arms over his chest again, his expression one of annoyance. "No, I'm not carrying a grudge against her. Do I want to get back together? Sure. But only because I miss her. She was the best thing that ever happened to me and I stupidly let her go. But hey, if she's not interested, then she's not interested."

Luke stared at Feeney, not bothering to hide the protectiveness he felt toward Megan. "When did you arrive here in Crystal Lake?" he asked.

Jake hesitated, obviously aware that Luke could verify whatever he said with the motel. "A couple of days ago. Thursday, I think."

Luke raised a brow. Interesting. "And you didn't contact Megan until tonight?"

"That's right."

"Why not?"

Feeney shifted impatiently. "Look, why all the questions? I don't have any reason to harm Megan or to break into her motel room. I didn't even know she was staying here. If you want to search my room, go ahead." He stepped back invitingly.

Luke accepted the silent dare, glancing back over his shoulder to signal one of the deputies to come over. The two men went into Jake Feeney's motel room and looked around.

They didn't find a razor blade or any evidence that he'd been inside Megan's room. There was a hint of alcohol on Feeney's breath, verifying his story that he'd spent the night at Barry's Pub drinking.

"Which car is yours?" Luke asked, when his deputy finished the search.

"I have a rental, it's that dark blue Toyota Camry."

"Why are you driving a rental car?"

Feeney's mask of indifference slipped. "It's not a crime and it's none of your business."

"It is if you don't want me to impound the car as potential evidence," Luke countered.

Feeney flushed with anger. "You can't do that."

"Sure I can. This isn't Chicago. You're on my turf now."

Feeney wrestled his temper under control. "I crashed my car about a month ago. I don't need a car in Chicago, I can use the subway to get to work. But to come up here, I needed a ride. So I rented the car."

Trouble at work, a wrecked car. There was definitely more to Feeney's story than what he was saying. "I need you to come down to our headquarters some time after eleven o'clock in the morning," Luke said, closing his notebook.

"What for?" Feeney demanded.

"Because I want to check out your story and I may have more questions for you."

His scowl deepened. "But I'm not under arrest."

Not yet, Luke thought. "No." He decided not to mention Liza's murder. For one thing, if Feeney had been in town since Thursday, he'd have heard about it by now. And for another, if by some miracle he hadn't heard about it, he wanted his reaction on tape.

"Don't leave town," Luke repeated. "If you don't show up tomorrow I will issue a warrant for your arrest."

The fake charm was back as Feeney smiled. "I'll be there, Sheriff. I don't have anything to hide."

Luke seriously doubted that, but he took a step back

and then waited as Feeney went back into his motel room and closed the door.

Heading back to his squad car, he debated how much to tell Megan. And what to do with her. Clearly, she was in danger. And he only had two deputies on staff during the night shifts.

"What happened?" she asked, the moment he slid behind the wheel.

"He claims he's been in town since Thursday, and that jibes with what the motel clerk told me. But I think there's more to his story."

Megan frowned. "Jake isn't a murderer, Luke."

He didn't necessarily agree. "It's almost four in the morning. I need to do some work down at headquarters. There's a small office with a cot at the end of the hall if you want to rest there for a while. It will take me some time to arrange for round-the-clock protection for you."

She hesitated for a moment before nodding slowly. "I guess that will be fine. But if you don't mind, I'd rather help with the investigation. If you have leads or something you need followed up on, I'd be happy to pitch in."

He considered her offer. As an experienced crime scene investigator, her input would be invaluable. Yet if the killer had targeted her for some reason, could her involvement actually jeopardize his case? Considering she had become involved, he should start examining the links between her old case and this new one.

"Let me think about what you can help with," he finally agreed. "And if you don't mind, I'm going to run home first, to get my uniform." And to talk to Sam.

"No problem,"

He headed for the highway, anxious to get back to his office so he could follow up on Jake Feeney.

The more he thought about the guy's story, the more implausible it seemed. If he was here to see Megan, why wait until Saturday night to track her down? What had the guy been doing since Thursday? They hadn't seen any fishing or boating gear in the motel room.

Luke didn't like the Feeney angle. Didn't like it at all.

About a half mile from his home, his headlights picked up a lone figure walking alongside the road. As he drew closer, he sucked in a harsh breath.

Megan had noticed the figure too. "Is that Sam?" she asked incredulously.

"Yes," he replied grimly, slowing down as he approached his son. He had no idea why Sam happened to be walking along the side of the road at roughly four-twenty in the morning.

And worse, he hadn't seen his son since nine-thirty at night. So where in the world had Sam been for the past seven hours?

SIX

Luke pulled over to the side of the road, rolled down the window and glared at his son. "Get in."

For a moment he thought Sam was going to argue, since they were literally a half mile from the house, but Sam wordlessly pulled open the back door to the squad car and climbed in.

In his rearview mirror, Luke could see how Sam glanced at Megan before directing his gaze out the window. He belatedly realized his son didn't know anything about Megan. "Sam, this is Megan O'Ryan. She's a crime scene investigator from Chicago. Megan, this is my son, Sam."

Megan swiveled in her seat to make eye contact with Sam. She smiled. "Hi, Sam, it's nice to meet you."

"Likewise," Sam murmured, surprising Luke with his polite response.

Luke wrestled with the instinct to demand to know where Sam had been. Was it possible his son had walked all the way into town and broken into Megan's room to leave the beer bottle?

He didn't want to believe it. No matter how sullen and angry Sam had become lately, he just couldn't believe his son was guilty of burglary or worse, murder.

But he had to admit, the fact that Sam was always disappearing, apparently without an alibi for the time frame of at least two crimes, cast a nasty cloud of suspicion over his son's head.

There were plenty of people in town who'd labeled Sam as trouble, the same way Megan had the first time she saw him. And even though he and his son had lived in Crystal Lake for eighteen months, many still considered them outsiders.

He believed his son was innocent, but feared others in the area were just as likely to point the finger at him. Especially if they knew his son had a criminal record. Thankfully, juvenile records were protected.

But they could be revealed by a court order from a judge.

"Are you helping my dad with Liza's murder?" Sam asked Megan. Again, Luke was surprised his son was even trying to make conversation.

Apparently, Sam was willing to talk to anyone but him.

Her smile was strained. "I'm trying."

Luke pulled into his driveway and then turned off the car. When his son climbed out, he spoke up. "Sam, I'd like a word with you if you don't mind."

Sam grunted—a response Luke chose to believe was reluctant agreement.

Megan glanced at him. "Luke, do you mind if I use your bathroom?"

"Of course not." Luke led the way inside and showed her where the bathroom was located, off the kitchen. He went back into the living room where Sam stood with his arms crossed over his chest defensively. Luke didn't smell any alcohol on his son's breath, and he tried to take that as a good sign. "What time did you leave the house?" Luke asked.

Sam shrugged. "I don't know."

He tempered a flash of impatience. "Look, Sam, I'm asking for a reason. There was a break-in down at the motel about two-thirty this morning. I'd like to know what time you left and where you've been."

The flash of surprise in Sam's eyes was reassuring. "I don't know exactly what time I left. But I walked down to the south shore for a bonfire. And then I walked back home."

Luke stared at Sam, trying to read his son's face. As much as he wanted to believe Sam's story, it seemed odd that one of his buddies wouldn't have come and picked him up rather than making him walk.

"Who was at the bonfire?" Luke asked.

This time Sam averted his gaze. "There was a group of us. What difference does it make? I wasn't anywhere near the motel."

Luke wanted names and exact details, especially if they'd been drinking. He didn't smell anything on his son's breath, but then again, if Sam had been walking for a couple of hours the alcohol could be out of his system by now. Out of the corner of his eye he noticed Megan hovering in the kitchen, obviously not wanting to interrupt.

"Write down the names for me," he said finally. He decided to leave the alcohol issue alone for now, only because he really wanted the names of the kids who were present and he suspected Sam wouldn't give them up if Luke came down too hard. "Sam, I can't protect you if you aren't honest with me."

Sam stared at the toes of his black boots for a long moment. "Fine. I'll write them down."

Luke couldn't hide his relief. "Thanks. It's important, or I wouldn't ask."

Sam gave a jerky nod and then disappeared down the hall toward his room without saying anything more. Luke gazed after him for a moment. Was it possible Sam was actually beginning to take this mess seriously? He certainly hoped so. His son had enough problems without adding any more.

Luke quickly changed into his work uniform and then came back out to the kitchen where Megan waited patiently. She sipped a glass of ice water, her expression thoughtful. "Ready?" he asked.

She nodded, rose to her feet and polished off the water before setting the empty glass in the sink.

He debated knocking on his son's door to get the names, but decided that information could wait. He needed to focus on Feeney for right now.

Megan must have sensed what he was thinking. "Everything okay with Sam?" she asked.

"Yeah, for the moment." As they headed out to his squad car, he changed the subject. "Did Feeney explain why he wanted to get back together with you?"

She glanced at him in surprise, their gazes locking over the roof of the car for a long moment before she broke the connection by sliding into the passenger seat. "No, but then again, I didn't ask. Mostly because it really wouldn't matter one way or the other, my answer would have been the same."

A flicker of satisfaction eased the tension in his shoulders. "Apparently he's had some trouble at work. I'm going to do a little digging to find out more."

She frowned a bit and nodded. "And what would you like me to do?"

He flashed a wry grin. "I suppose it's too much to ask that you get some much-needed rest?"

"I'm too keyed up to sleep."

He suppressed a sigh, wishing she would simply let him take care of her. But Megan had an independent stubborn streak. "Okay, then maybe I'll have you go through the information on Paul Sherman again from the trial. Maybe there's someone close to him who is carrying a grudge against you for locking him up."

Megan nodded slowly. "I can do that."

"Good." He pulled his vehicle into the parking lot and led the way inside the sheriff's department headquarters. At this time of night, the place was pretty much deserted except for Abby, the night shift dispatcher.

"Abby, this is Megan O'Ryan," he said, making quick introductions. "Megan, this is Abby, the night shift dispatcher for the county."

"Nice to meet you," Abby said.

Megan walked over to shake her hand. "Nice to meet you, too."

"Megan is going to stay in the back room for a while," he informed the dispatcher. "I told her to make herself at home."

"Sure, no problem, boss."

He grimaced a bit. Abby knew he hated being called "boss," but since that was how she'd always addressed his predecessor, the habit had been hard to break.

After getting cups of coffee from the coffeepot that he kept stocked with decent coffee, no station sludge allowed, they made their way to his office.

"Okay, here are the transcripts from the trial," he

said, handing Megan a huge binder full of paper. He led the way down the hall to the small room that was used as an office/sleep room. There was a desk with an older-model computer and a sparsely made cot. When Megan sat down in the chair behind the desk, staring at the binder, he hesitated. "Are you sure you're okay to do this? Because you don't have to help."

"I'll be fine," she said hastily.

"If you're sure. Otherwise, if you want to catch up on some sleep, that's fine too."

"I'll review the information first." Megan glanced up at him, the familiar stubborn angle to her chin making him want to smile. "Thanks for bringing me here, Luke. Being part of the action is much better than sitting in some motel room all alone."

The urge to cross over and gather her close was almost overwhelming. He slid his hands into his pockets as a reminder to keep them to himself. He was still bothered by her earlier comment. God hadn't given up on her, but she'd clearly given up on Him. But Luke wasn't sure how to broach the subject of her faith, or lack of, so he stepped back. "You're welcome," he said gruffly. "Call me if you need anything."

"I will."

He turned on his heel and strode back to his office before he did something he'd regret.

Like kiss her.

It took him a while to get in touch with the Chicago P.D. district that Jake Feeney worked for. And even then, it took another hour for the lieutenant in charge to get back to him. That conversation was brief, the lieutenant basically telling him he had to wait for Feeney's superior to come in.

At seven in the morning, his phone finally rang. The caller was the Chicago chief of police, not Feeney's direct supervisor.

"Sheriff Torretti? I understand you're looking for information on one of my men."

Luke knew he had to step carefully or these guys would clam up and he'd never get anywhere. "Thanks for returning my phone call, Chief. I only wanted to verify what Officer Feeney told me. I'm investigating a series of crimes here in Crystal Lake and one of the victims happens to be Officer Feeney's ex-fiancée. When I questioned him as to why he was here in Crystal Lake, he told me he took a few days off because he's had some trouble at work. He also told me that he was driving a rental car because he'd been in a motor vehicle crash about a month ago. Are you willing to verify both of those claims for me?"

There was a long pause on the other end of the line, and Luke's heart sank when he sensed he was about to be stonewalled. "All I can tell you at this time is that Officer Feeney is on paid leave. And yes, he was in a car crash recently. I'm happy to send you the police report."

"I would appreciate that, Chief." Luke drummed his fingers on the desktop, trying to figure out a way to get more out of the tight-lipped chief of police. His gut was telling him that there was much more to this story; why else would he be getting a call from the chief himself? "You mentioned how Officer Feeney is on paid leave. Can you tell me if his conduct on duty is being investigated?"

Another long pause. "No, I'm afraid I can't tell you anything about his leave. However, if you want to send me the information on what crimes you're investigating, I'd be happy to review the details to see if there is any possible overlap to what is going on here."

"All right," he agreed slowly. He couldn't really afford not to follow up on a potential link, even though he'd rather be the one reviewing the details instead of the other way around. He rattled off his fax number for the report on the car crash and then took the Chicago PD fax number down as well.

True to the chief's word, the report on Feeney's car crash came through the fax in less than five minutes.

He quickly scanned the information. Jake Feeney had been found to be at fault and had been issued several tickets. No wonder he was in trouble at work, considering the seriousness of the offenses.

One ticket was issued for failing to yield to the right of way. One for driving under the influence. And one for reckless endangerment. According to the police report, the victim in the other car had been taken to the hospital for treatment of serious injuries. Luke had to assume that the victim hadn't died, or Feeney would be up for reckless homicide instead.

Definitely trouble. And several good reasons to be on paid leave. He was surprised Feeney's license hadn't been revoked. Hadn't the case gone to court yet?

No, the court date was still pending. And as he looked closer, he realized the date of the accident was just two weeks ago, not a month. Feeney had lied about the time frame.

Interesting. What else had he lied about?

Megan opened the binder of transcripts with trepidation. She could do this.

She had to do this.

The killer had targeted her for a reason. Luke might think Jake Feeney was involved, but she didn't.

No, the answer was likely buried here in the past. The similarities of the murders meant they were connected somehow. She was the link.

The idea was chilling.

Megan tried to concentrate, but as she began to read, her eyes burned with fatigue and unshed tears.

Reading the cold hard facts surrounding her sister's murderer was more difficult than she'd imagined. She'd blocked so much out of her mind from sheer necessity.

When tears kept trickling down her cheeks, she wiped them away with an impatient hand. She tipped her head back and stared at the ceiling of the tiny office. Okay, at this rate she'd never get through any of the transcripts to be of any help.

Maybe she needed to focus her efforts on Paul Sherman himself. Hadn't Luke suggested that very thing? Sherman was the most logical person to hold a grudge against her. Especially the way he kept claiming he was innocent.

Her DNA testing had proved otherwise. And a jury of his peers had found him guilty. During her testimony, his cold stare had never wavered. Yes, she could certainly imagine Paul Sherman holding a deep grudge against her. Which meant that someone close to him might be seeking revenge.

She took several deep breaths, struggling to get a grip on her emotions. Katie was gone and nothing was going to bring her sister back. But she could help Liza's family. Her parents deserved closure too.

With renewed determination, she opened the binder and searched for the personal information on Paul

Sherman. She remembered how the prosecuting attorney had poked into the guy's past.

She skimmed the documents till she found what she was looking for. Paul Sherman was an only child. His mother had left him when he was six and Paul grew up with his abusive father. Paul had demonstrated violent tendencies at an early age, no doubt learned from his father, as evidenced by the fights he'd gotten into as a teenager. He'd spent time in a juvenile facility for aggravated assault at sixteen. At the time of the murders, he was twenty-eight years old and seemed to be putting his life back together, taking night classes at the local university.

The same university her sister, Katie, had attended.

She took another deep breath, shying away from thoughts about Katie. Paul's abusive father was dead. There was no evidence Paul had fathered any children, and even if he had, the child wouldn't have been old enough to avenge Paul by committing copycat murders. Paul had a cousin on his father's side, a man two years younger, by the name of Kyle Sherman. Megan flagged that name as a possibility, although there wasn't any indication that Kyle and Paul had ever been close.

As she sat there, she found herself wondering about Paul's mother. Reaching over to the computer, she booted up the device and waited for the ancient equipment to load. She tested the internet access and discovered the computer was connected to the sheriff's department network. The other applications were password protected, but she could access the internet without needing a password.

After nearly an hour of digging, she discovered Paul Sherman's mother had remarried and had another son.

Everett Dobrowski was Paul Sherman's half-brother, and he'd just turned twenty-one.

She added Everett Dobrowski's name to the list next to Kyle Sherman's name. Both remote possibilities, all things considered, but at least they were leads to follow up on.

Excited to have something to show to Luke, she took the information she'd found and headed back down the hall to the main office area.

Luke was sitting behind his desk, his expression intent, and for a moment she simply stared at him, her heart skipping a beat.

She'd only known him for a few days—why was she so hyper-aware of him? She tried to tell herself it was just because they were working so closely together on this case.

But she couldn't really make herself believe it.

He glanced up then, as if sensing her presence. She flushed, hoping he hadn't realized she was standing there staring at him.

"Hi. I found two distant relatives to Sherman who might be carrying out a grudge against me." She walked in and set the information on his desk. "They're remote possibilities, since there is no evidence that Sherman might be close to either of them, but it's worth a shot."

"Great work," Luke told her. "Any other close friends?"

"Nothing yet, but I'll keep looking."

Luke nodded. "And here's what I found out about your former boyfriend."

She took the report he offered, scanning the information quickly. When she read about the three citations, her stomach knotted. "I had no idea," she murmured.

"He's in trouble, that's for sure. But the chief of police isn't going to give me any more information."

She wasn't sure what to say. Jake hadn't overindulged much while they were together, but maybe something else had happened. "He did a lot of work in the south side, where gang violence was running rampant. Maybe the stress of everything had gotten to him?"

Luke's gaze bored into hers. "Megan, do you still have feelings for Jake Feeney?"

She blushed but shook her head. "No. Not the way you're thinking."

"Then do you mind telling me why you keep jumping to his defense? You were the one who told me that someone wearing a ball cap has been following you. Jake is here in a rental car and has a ball cap. Not only that, but he shows up without warning, two days before making contact with you." There was a flash of annoyance in his eyes. "I just don't understand why you're defending him."

She could understand Luke's frustration. "I don't know, exactly. I guess deep down, I don't want to believe the guy I once dated is capable of murder."

"He claims you were engaged to be married."

She could tell by his terse tone that he wasn't happy to have found out from Jake. "He gave me a ring, and I was so shocked, I didn't know what to say," she explained. "I did agree to marry him, honestly thinking that there was plenty of time to change my mind, but it didn't matter because our engagement only lasted a week. My sister was murdered and that pretty much ended our relationship."

"I see." Luke sighed. "Okay, so we have more suspects now than we had a few hours ago. That's progress."

"Boss?" Megan turned to see Abby standing in the doorway. "I'm leaving now, but Mayor Ganzer is here to see you."

"Send him in. Stay," he said, when Megan edged toward the door. "We're going to discuss the need for police protection for you."

She nodded, and stood awkwardly near the door as the mayor, a tall, round man with a ruddy complexion, walked into the room. The mayor was dressed formally for a Sunday, wearing a pair of dress pants and a short-sleeved dress shirt and a loud tie. "Sheriff? You've put in a request for more overtime? What's going on? Has there been a break in the case?"

Luke stood and quickly introduced her to the mayor. "Yes. Liga's killer is targeting Megan," Luke said. He quickly summarized the events surrounding the break-in at the motel. "She's also being followed. It's clear Megan is in danger."

Mayor Ed Ganzer's red face darkened and his gaze narrowed. "She's a crime scene investigator, right?"

It was on the tip of her tongue to correct him. *Former* crime scene investigator.

"Yes," Luke acknowledged.

"That means she's trained to defend herself. And you pointed out that the killer broke into her room to leave evidence, nothing more. He had the chance to hurt her and he didn't."

This time, Luke didn't respond.

"We don't have the department funds to approve overtime to have someone watch over her," the mayor continued in a firm tone. "Our budget is strained at the seams the way it is."

Luke's expression turned grim. "Are you denying my request?"

"Yes." She wasn't surprised when the mayor avoided her gaze, focusing on Luke instead as if she weren't standing right next to him in the room. "There's no evidence that she's in mortal danger, and she's trained to defend herself. I'm sorry, but at this point, she's on her own."

SEVEN

Megan slipped out of Luke's office while he was still arguing with Mayor Ganzer. She was so exhausted that the meaning of what had just happened sank into her numb brain slowly.

No police protection would be approved

She was on her own.

She gave her head a little shake to help clear out the cobwebs. Okay, so being on her own was nothing new; she'd taken care of her sister after their parents had died. She was strong and independent. But somehow she'd let down her guard with Luke. And she'd begun to believe he'd always protect her. Or at least be there for her.

Disconcerting to think that maybe she wasn't as strong and independent as she thought.

Instead of going back down the hall to the tiny office, she headed outside, needing some fresh air. The sun was out, and even at nine in the morning, the temperature was rising. Standing outside of the sheriff's department headquarters, where the rest of the world went about their normal daily activities, she told herself the mayor was probably right. She didn't need 24/7 police protection.

Although someone to watch over her at night would

have been nice, considering that was when the killer tended to strike.

Desperate for a break from the murder case, she walked across the parking lot to the road. She heard the melodic sound of church bells and saw a white church steeple towering above the trees, not far down the highway.

Instinctively, she headed that way, even though she hadn't been inside a church in well over a year. Since Katie's murder. Since she'd felt as if God had stopped listening.

Since she'd stopped praying altogether.

It dawned on her as she approached the church, where she could see people calling out greetings to each other as they went inside, that the reason the mayor was dressed nicely was likely because he'd planned on attending services. She glanced down at her jeans with a grimace. Too bad she wasn't. Refusing to let that stop her, she ducked inside the church.

She quickly slid into a seat in the very back corner, hoping no one would notice her jeans and tennis shoes. She clasped her hands in her lap and bowed her head.

Almost immediately, a sense of peace settled over her.

Why had she waited so long to come here? Why hadn't she understood that maybe she'd been the one to give up on God, not the other way around? She thought of Katie's death and tears pricked her eyes.

She'd been so angry at God for so long. And suddenly, she didn't have the energy to hang on to that anger any longer. She still missed Katie desperately, but maybe she needed to consider what their pastor had told her. How Katie might be in a better place.

A sense of peace washed through her entire body, and she knew she'd made the right choice in coming here today.

Just before the pastor began his service, Luke slid into the church pew beside her. She glanced up at him in surprise. He smiled, covered her hand briefly with his, and then turned his attention to the pastor as he began to speak.

With Luke beside her, all her senses went on high alert. Sitting beside him made her feel strangely as if they were a couple. Maybe because she'd never attended church with a man. Jake hadn't been one to attend services.

As the pastor spoke, his words resonated deep inside. Especially the quote from Psalms 27:1, The Lord is my light and my salvation—whom shall I fear? The Lord is the stronghold of my life—of whom should I be afraid?

He didn't preach so much as he had a conversation with them. When the service was over, she found she was strangely reluctant to leave. She slowly rose to her feet and filed out of the building with the other parishioners. Luke surprised her by staying right beside her.

When he headed back toward the sheriff's headquarters, she stopped him with a hand on his arm. "I'm not ready to go back just yet. Would you mind if we took a short walk? Or if you're too busy, I'll just go on my own."

"No, I'm not too busy for a walk." He veered off to the right, leading her down a path through some trees. "I think after everything you've been through, you definitely deserve a break."

"Not just me," she corrected. "We both deserve a

break." Luke had been putting in many hours on the investigation, she knew. And he had Sam to deal with. She'd tried not to listen early this morning as Luke and his son had talked, but it was clear that Luke had his hands full with Sam.

They strolled at an easy pace, side by side, their fingers occasionally brushing. She was keenly aware of the slightest touch. They didn't talk much, but the silence wasn't the least bit uncomfortable.

So different from the times she'd spent with Jake. Why was it so easy now to see how wrong she and Jake were for each other? Being with Luke like this felt right.

"Do you attend church services often?" she asked, breaking the companionable silence.

"Yes, at least I have been for the past two years. After my wife died, I tried to drown my sorrows in a bottle of whiskey, but of course that only made things worse."

She winced, thinking of what he now faced with Sam's underage drinking. "I'm sorry for your loss," she murmured.

He flashed a lopsided smile. "Thank you. Those were some dark days, and I obviously lost sight of my faith. It wasn't until I hit rock bottom, nearly losing my job and my son to social services, that I managed to pull myself together."

She sucked in a harsh breath. He'd almost lost his son? She couldn't imagine. "Oh, Luke."

He stared forward, seemingly lost in memories of the past. "My faith helped ground me in reality. Except that once I got my life back on track, I discovered Sam was running with a bad group of kids, gang member wannabe's."

Oh, no. Her heart squeezed in her chest. Poor Sam. And poor Luke.

"When he got arrested for armed robbery after holding up a clerk at knifepoint, I decided to move away from Milwaukee and to come here, to Crystal Lake."

She was humbled by the way he'd managed to pull himself together after his wife died, and felt a sense of shame at how she couldn't seem to get past her sister's death. Although attending church this morning had provided a sense of peace she hadn't felt in a long time. "That was a good decision on your part," she said.

"Was it?" Luke grimaced and shook his head. "I wish I could be so sure. You can probably tell by now how my relationship with Sam has suffered. And his drinking scares me. Yet if we'd stayed in Milwaukee, I truly believe things would be worse. Much worse." He let out his breath in a heavy sigh. "All I can do at this point is to keep trying to connect with Sam and pray for the Lord to watch over him."

She was startled to hear him say that he prayed. Not so much that he did pray, but that he wasn't shy about talking about it.

"God never abandons us, you know," Luke said softly. "We're the ones that sometimes abandon Him. Don't give up on your faith, Megan."

Since she'd come to that realization herself, she couldn't argue. "I'm trying not to," she admitted.

"Good. I keep hoping Sam will realize the same thing." Luke's smile was sad.

She and Katie had attended church while growing up, and even after their parents had died, they had continued to attend services when they could. But how many times had she truly opened herself up to God? She knew attending services wasn't enough. Maybe she needed to reestablish her relationship with God through prayer.

"I'm sure he'll come around," she said, shaking off her thoughts and belatedly picking up the thread of the conversation. "Teenagers can be difficult."

"Yeah. I know."

"Deep down, Sam loves you."

"I'm not so sure about that. Sometimes I think he hates me." Luke was quiet for a moment before he changed the subject. "About what happened back in my office, I wanted to let you know that the mayor and I reached a compromise. You can stay in the small office, sleeping on the cot at night. There's always a few deputies coming and going and the dispatcher is there as well, so you won't ever be alone. That way, we can keep an eye on you, even without overtime."

She digested the offer. Wasn't someone watching over her at night what she'd hoped for? The compromise was better than what she'd expected. "If you're sure I won't be in the way."

"Trust me, you won't be in the way," he hastily assured her. "And I would sleep easier, knowing you were someplace safe."

She was touched by his admission.

"The cot won't be the most comfortable thing to sleep on but it's not that bad. I've used it myself. There's a bathroom, but no shower, unfortunately." Luke flashed a guilty glance.

No shower. Ugh. Oh well, she'd handle it. Surely she could go home to shower during the daytime. And who knows, maybe she'd only need to stay for a few days. "I guess that would work," she agreed.

Luke's relief was evident on his features. "Thank you."

She glanced up at him in surprise. "I think I'm supposed to be the one thanking you."

He laughed, and the sound was rusty, as if he didn't laugh very often. "Megan, you're amazing. I was fully prepared for you to be extremely upset with me."

"I'm not upset," she assured him.

They turned back toward the sheriff's department. "I want you to know," Luke continued, "I'm not going to rest until I have this guy behind bars."

"I know." Surprisingly, she trusted Luke. His abilities and his dedication. "I believe you."

"The biggest holdup on this case is going to be getting the evidence processed in the Madison crime lab. If you have any strings to pull in order to get my crime scene evidence processed more quickly, I'd appreciate it."

For a moment she felt a strange sense of déjà vu. She'd done the same thing, pulling in favors, after Katie's death. Her friend Raoul Lee had helped her last time. He was still in Chicago, the last time she'd checked.

"I'll see what I can do," she promised. "I'm only temporarily on staff in Madison, to help get the backlog of DNA testing caught up. But maybe a friend of mine can help."

Luke glanced at her. "I don't suppose you can process the DNA for me on that beer bottle we found in your motel room."

"I don't know." She'd helped with the DNA testing on Katie's murder, but that was a little different in that she was related to the victim. Not actually *the* victim.

"Probably not, since the bottle was found in my motel room and really needs to be tested to make sure nothing on it matches my DNA."

Luke let out another sigh. "Yeah, that's what I was afraid of."

They walked back inside the sheriff's department headquarters and Luke was immediately engulfed in activity. Everyone wanted a few minutes of his time.

He glanced at her, as if feeling bad for abandoning her, and she flashed a small smile. "It's okay, I understand. But my car is still at the motel, so if someone could give me a ride, I'd appreciate it."

Luke nodded, but before he could give anyone the directive to take her home, he was interrupted once again when Jake Feeney walked in.

"I'm here for my interview, Sheriff." Jake's eyes widened in shock when he noticed Megan. "Megan? What on earth are you doing here?"

Luke glanced between Megan and Jake, noticing how Megan looked extremely uncomfortable. But before he could intervene, she took control of the situation.

"My motel room was broken into last night," she said, as if she didn't already know that Jake had been questioned by Luke a few hours earlier. "I had to come and make a statement."

Luke cleared his throat. "Deputy Frank Rawson is ready to drive you back to the motel, Ms. O'Ryan," he said, as he signaled Frank with his gaze. He was glad Megan hadn't indicated she was here helping to work on the murder case. At this point, he wanted to keep that tidbit of information under wraps.

Frank obliged by stepping forward. "This way, Ms. O'Ryan."

"Thank you," she murmured, following Frank outside.

Luke turned his attention to Jake Feeney. "Over there," he said, indicating their one and only interview room. "I'll be with you in a moment."

He went to get a tape recorder and notepaper before returning to the interview room. After taking a seat across from Feeney, he turned on the tape recorder. "This interview with Jake Feeney is being recorded at eleven thirty-five in the morning on Sunday."

Jake grimaced. "Is that really necessary?"

Luke narrowed his gaze. "Are you protesting the recording of this interview? Do you want to retain a lawyer?"

"No, I don't need a lawyer. I didn't do anything wrong! Go ahead and record the conversation, I don't care."

"Tell me again, what brought you to Crystal Lake, Wisconsin."

Jake sighed. "I had some trouble at work. I was told to take a few days off, so I decided to come up here to see Megan. We used to be engaged, and I was stupid enough to break things off with her. She was the best thing in my life, and I hoped to convince her to give me another chance."

"What time did you arrive in Crystal Lake?"

"Thursday, about three o'clock in the afternoon. You can verify that, since I checked into the motel right when I arrived."

Luke made note of the time. "You arrived on Thursday and checked into your motel room at three. What did you do then?"

Jake didn't shift in his seat or look at all nervous. If he was guilty, he sure wasn't showing any of the typical signs. "I called Megan, but her phone was off, because the call went straight to her voice mail."

"Did you leave a message?"

"No. I thought it might be better to surprise her. So I asked around, trying to find out where she lived. But no one seemed to know."

Because the locals still referred to Megan's cabin as the Dartmouth place. "So then what did you do?"

"I figured I'd take my lieutenant's advice and relax a bit. Went down to the docks, rented a boat and took a spin out on the lake."

Luke's interest peaked at that. Liza's murder happened on Friday night, or early Saturday morning, they still didn't have the final report from the medical examiner. The fact that Feeney rented a boat on Thursday was very interesting. "How many days did you rent the boat for?"

"Just twenty-four hours. I had to return the boat by three o'clock on Friday because it was already rented for the weekend."

So he didn't have the boat on the night Liza was killed. Somewhat disappointed, he asked, "Where were you on Friday night?"

"I hung out at Barry's Pub most of Friday night. Shot some pool and that was about it. I left at midnight or twelve-thirty."

His pulse kicked up. No alibi for the time frame of the murder? "Did you leave alone? Can anyone verify your story?"

"My story?" Jake's eyes widened and then narrowed suspiciously. "Wait a minute, this is about that girl, isn't it? The teenager who was killed? I heard about it on Saturday at the pub. You can't seriously think I'm a possible suspect?"

Luke kept his expression neutral. "Answer the question. Can anyone verify your story? Did you leave the pub alone on Friday night?"

"Yes, someone can verify my story," Feeney said, his eyes glinting with anger. "If you must know, I didn't leave alone, I left with a woman I met that night. Her name was Krista. Krista Whitney, or maybe it was Krista White."

Luke jotted down the name. "Where was Krista staying? At the same motel?"

"No, she was with a group of friends and said they were staying at the Crystal Lake Campground, which is apparently a few miles out of town. There were four or five people in her group. I didn't really pay much attention."

Verifying Feeney's story wouldn't be easy. It was possible that the woman he'd met wasn't registered with the campground; often it was just one of the members of a group who registered. He'd have to ask Frank to check it out. "Did anyone else see you and this woman go into your motel room?"

"I don't know. Maybe. It wasn't like I announced it down Main Street." Feeney's charade of cooperation was wearing thin. He was growing more and more annoyed as he glared at Luke. "Look, I'll give you a DNA sample if that will help clear me of the murder. And the break-in to Megan's motel room. But I'm telling you, I didn't know the girl who died. I didn't kill her. You have the wrong guy."

Maybe. Maybe not. "Why did you wait until Saturday night to call Megan?" Luke asked, changing tactics a bit. "Seems odd for you to pick up some strange woman in a bar, when supposedly you came here to get back together with Megan."

"Yeah. Look, I'd rather Megan didn't know anything about Krista, okay? I mean, she didn't mean anything to me. It was just one of those things. Megan is the one I really care about. When I was with Megan, things were going great. After we broke up, my life suddenly went downhill. I thought if we got back together, maybe things would start turning around for me."

The guy was completely clueless. Apparently he wasn't the type to take responsibility for his own actions. And as far as not telling Megan, Luke wasn't promising anything. "You still didn't answer my question."

Feeney sighed. "I don't know, okay? I guess I knew my chances with Megan were slim to none. After I spent the night with Krista, I knew I'd made a mistake. I called Megan the next night, and she did meet with me. But only for one drink, and during that time is when she told me she wasn't ready for a relationship. You know the rest."

Luke stared at Jake Feeney for a long moment, trying to decide how much of his story he really believed. He was bothered by the fact that Megan didn't tell Feeney to take a hike. She'd taken the easy way out, telling him she wasn't ready for a relationship.

Or was it possible she really wasn't ready for a relationship? And why was he disturbed by that thought?

"How long are you planning to stay in town?" he finally asked.

"I was planning to leave today. In fact, I've already checked out of my motel room."

Luke didn't like it, but he couldn't see how he could force the issue either. He didn't have enough to arrest Feeney, no matter how much he didn't like the guy. "I need your contact information, in case I have more questions."

Jake reluctantly rattled off his cell number

"You should also know, I've been in touch with your chief of police and know a little bit about the trouble you've been in. If for some reason you don't return my calls, I won't hesitate to go to him again."

That news obviously bothered Feeney, judging by the way his jaw tightened and he clenched his fists. Luke watched calmly as the Chicago cop reined in his temper. "Anything else, Sheriff?" he asked testily.

"No. You're free to go." Luke shut off the tape recorder and rose to his feet. "I'll be in touch if I have anything else."

For a moment it looked as if Feeney wanted to say something more, but he must have thought better of it and simply turned and walked away. Luke followed more slowly. His deputy, Frank Rawson, was just coming back from driving Megan to the motel.

"What do you think? Is he a viable suspect?" Frank asked, watching Feeney as he stalked out of the building.

"I'm not sure, we need to check out a few details of his story," Luke admitted. Unfortunately, he found himself inclined to believe Feeney. The guy was a clueless jerk, but Luke couldn't buy the theory that he'd murdered Liza. Although his connection to Megan was worth investigating further. But at the moment, he had another, more pressing concern. "Do you have a few minutes to come into my office?"

Frank nodded. "Sure." He looked a little surprised when Luke shut the door and then retreated to sit behind his desk. "What's up?"

Luke sat there, looking at the one man on the force that he trusted implicitly, trying to choose his words carefully. He'd already put this off for too long. "There is another potential suspect that I need you to interview for me," he said finally.

"Sure. Who's that?"

He stared down at his desk for a long moment and then lifted his head, forcing himself to meet Frank's curious gaze. "My son, Sam."

EIGHT

Megan was grateful Deputy Frank had driven her back to the motel, so she could collect the rest of her belongings, check out and pick up her car. Frank stayed beside her the entire time, and when she went to the tiny motel office to check out, he insisted on taking care of the bill.

As soon as he'd paid her tab, Deputy Frank had tipped his hat and left, driving back toward headquarters. Instead of going straight home, Megan stopped at the diner for a late breakfast.

"Hi, sweetie, what can I get you?" Josie asked.

As she was suddenly starving, she ordered the lumberjack meal, which consisted of pancakes, eggs, bacon and fried potatoes.

She put a good dent in the meal, feeling better than she had in a long while. Maybe because of the time she'd spent with Luke.

Or maybe because she'd attended church for the first time in years.

Either way, she finally felt normal, almost lighthearted. As if she wasn't second-guessing herself. As if she was finally healing.

She pushed her empty plate away and left Josie a nice

tip before heading back outside. She drove home, and it wasn't until the moment she pulled into the long gravel driveway that her uneasiness returned.

Sitting in her car, she stared at her aunt's cabin. She hadn't been back since they'd identified her backyard as the location of Liza's murder. For some odd reason, she was loath to go inside.

Ridiculous, really. It was broad daylight on a sunny Sunday afternoon. With her driver's-side window open, she could hear the roaring sound of boat motors intermingled with laughter coming from the lake.

A perfectly normal Sunday. There was no reason to be afraid.

Maybe she wasn't as healed as she'd thought. Gathering her courage, Megan climbed out of the car. She walked around to the passenger side to pull out her overnight duffel bag.

She hadn't even taken one step when the crunch of tires against gravel had her spinning around so fast she nearly lost her balance and fell flat on her face.

Her heart pounding, she watched a dark blue Camry pull up behind her Sunfire. Her stomach clenched and goose bumps rippled up her arms when she recognized Jake Feeney.

How had Jake figured out where she lived?

He watched her warily as he slid out of the car. "Hi, Megan."

"Jake." She gripped the duffel tighter and lifted her chin. "What do you want? And how did you find me?"

"I was heading down Main Street when I saw you pull out of the motel parking lot. I turned around and followed you here."

He'd followed her today—had he followed her other times as well? And if so, why?

"I just stopped by to say goodbye," he continued, leaning on the open door. "I'm heading back to Chicago. Unless you've changed your mind about us?"

Was he kidding? The serious glint in his eye convinced her he wasn't. "No, I haven't changed my mind, Jake. You know as well as I do, we aren't suited for each other. We shouldn't have gotten engaged in the first place."

He stared at her for a long moment. "I don't necessarily agree," he said slowly. "But I can't think of anything to say to make you change your mind." He paused then added, "I hope we can at least remain friends."

Her muscles relaxed, the tenseness easing away. She smiled. "Sure, Jake. Of course we can be friends."

A corner of his mouth kicked up and he nodded. "Call me if you need anything, okay?"

"I will." She was tempted to ask him to come inside the cabin with her, just to make sure no one was waiting and hiding in there. But since she was concerned he'd misinterpret her request she bit back the urge. "Take care of yourself," she said instead as she turned away.

"Megan?"

She paused and swung back toward him. "Yes?"

"Where are you working now that you've left Chicago?"

"In Madison. I'm helping to get rid of the backlog of DNA testing. Why do you ask?"

He lifted a shoulder. "Just curious. When I saw you at the station, I thought maybe you were helping to investigate the murder."

She couldn't explain why she didn't tell him the truth.

"No, my only employment is with the Madison crime lab." Which was technically true. Her only paid job was in Madison. The time she'd spent with Luke was strictly volunteer work.

"I see. Well, goodbye, Megan." He finally slid back into the driver's seat of his car and gave her a nod as he backed out of the driveway.

She stared after him, perplexed. What difference did it make to Jake what she was working on? She made a mental note to ask Luke how his interview with Jake had gone.

Jake had distracted her enough that she wasn't as nervous walking into the cabin. A quick glance around showed that everything seemed to be as she'd left it. She walked through the entire cabin and checked every room just to be safe.

She saved her bedroom for last. She dropped her duffel bag on the bed and glanced around. Everything seemed fine.

As usual, she'd overreacted.

Her shoulders slumped with relief. Shaking her head at her own foolishness, she headed toward the tiny bathroom off her bedroom, intending to take a shower. After she was finished, she dried off with a towel. There was no fan, and the room was foggy.

Her heart jumped in her throat when she turned to face the mirror and saw the words written in the steam.

You can't stop me.

Megan waited impatiently for Luke outside her cabin. Despite the warmth of the sun, she was chilled to the bone.

She paced, unable to relax knowing Liza's murderer had been in her home. In her bedroom. In her bathroom.

Taunting her. Again.

When Luke's familiar vehicle pulled into her driveway, she had to force herself not to run and throw herself into his arms.

"Megan?" He jumped out of the car and strode toward her, his expression full of concern. "Are you all right?"

She swallowed hard. Tried to speak. But couldn't. She tried to nod.

"Megan," Luke murmured her name like a groan. And then he hauled her close, in a warm embrace.

She clung to him, with her cheek pressed against his chest, her arms locked around his waist. She knew she shouldn't be so weak as to need him this much. But at the same time, being held by Luke was extremely reassuring.

The killer couldn't get to her. Not with Luke's strong arms protectively wrapped around her.

She drew strength from Luke's embrace, holding onto him longer than was proper. He didn't let her go, though, until she loosened her grip.

Luke was looking down at her, his expression grave. "Show me," he murmured.

"I came in after talking to Jake," she began, as she headed back into the cabin.

"Wait," Luke said, capturing her arm and preventing her from going inside. "Feeney was here?"

"He came to say goodbye," she admitted.

Luke's gaze narrowed. "He told me he didn't know where you lived."

"He claims he saw me leaving the motel parking lot and followed me. I didn't come straight home after Deputy Frank dropped me off at the motel, I ate at the diner first."

Luke's intense gaze searched hers. "And that was all? He simply came to say goodbye?"

"Pretty much. He asked if I was helping you with the murder investigation and I managed to avoid a straight answer. I made it sound like I wasn't."

"Good." Luke didn't completely let go; instead he slid his hand down until he was holding hers. "Okay, tell me again exactly what you did."

She nodded. "I was nervous being here alone, so I pretty much went through the entire cabin, looking for anything that was out of place. I didn't notice any smears on the mirror, but after I took a shower, the message was clearly visible in the steam." Feeling somewhat self-conscious, she stopped in the middle of her bedroom and waved him toward the bathroom door. "Even without the fogged-up mirror, you can still make out the words."

"'You can't stop me,'" Luke said, reading them out loud. "We'll need to dust your mirror for fingerprints."

She'd thought of fingerprints too, although she seriously doubted they'd find anything. The murderer enjoyed toying with her and he wasn't going to make amateur mistakes. "The real problem is that I haven't been inside that bathroom since the night you dragged me out of bed to help you with Liza's body. He could have sneaked in here to leave that message at any time."

The idea was extremely unnerving.

"Or he could have purposefully left the message this

morning, as a welcome-home surprise for you," Luke said in a grim tone.

That thought was even less reassuring. Because it meant he knew everything about where she went and what she was doing.

"Pack up your stuff," Luke said, coming back into the bedroom. "I'm taking you with me back to the station."

She wasn't about to argue. This time she packed a bigger suitcase, rather than just an overnight duffel bag. While she packed, Luke went back outside and then returned with a fingerprint kit. He dusted the mirror, making the message stand out starkly.

"Nothing," he murmured when she came over to the doorway. "I should probably dust your entire house, but I have a feeling it would be a waste of time."

"I tend to agree. He might be a copycat killer, but he's not stupid. He's been covering his tracks very well, leaving only the bits of evidence that he wants us to find."

Luke let out his breath in a heavy sigh. "Are you ready to go?"

"Yes." She glanced around at the cabin that a few short days ago had been her refuge. Now she couldn't get out of there quickly enough.

Luke took her suitcase and waited for her to head outside. He quickly stashed her case in the trunk of his squad car and then held the passenger door open for her. She hesitated, glancing at her car. "I think it would be better if I drove myself, don't you?"

He hesitated, but then nodded. "I'll be right behind you," he promised.

The ride back to the sheriff's department headquarters didn't take long. The day-shift dispatcher was a younger woman named Cecilia. Luke quickly introduced her and then carried her suitcase down the hall to her office, setting the suitcase on the floor next to the cot. Somehow, the office seemed smaller than she'd remembered.

Maybe because it was clearly her home for the interim.

"Sheriff? Do you have a minute?" She recognized Frank's voice.

"Sure." Luke flashed a lopsided smile. "Make yourself at home."

She tried not to grimace. Since there wasn't a lot of room, she shoved the suitcase underneath the cot, and then sat down in the only chair in the room.

Now what? There had to be something she could do to help jump-start their case. Belatedly she remembered her promise to help expedite the evidence.

Raoul Lee, the chief microbiologist she'd worked with at the Chicago CSI lab, knew everyone in the business. He'd hired her and trained her. Mentored her. But it was Sunday, so he wouldn't be at work. Well, maybe he would be, since Raoul often worked at odd times of the day and night. Would he answer his cell phone? Maybe.

She still had his cell number programmed into her phone. Before the St. Patrick's Strangler had hit the streets of Chicago, Raoul had asked her out. She'd declined, explaining how she liked him as a friend, nothing more. He'd been upset at first, but then had taken her phone and punched in his phone number, telling her that she could call him anytime she'd changed her mind.

Shortly thereafter she'd met Jake, and Raoul had been angry when he found out. But then young victims were found in the parking lots of Irish pubs, so they all worked around the clock to bring the guy to justice.

After the trial, she'd avoided contact with her friends. She'd needed time to recuperate.

She stared down at the number indecisively. Raoul had seemed to get over his anger, but their friendship had certainly suffered. Would he be willing to help her out now? Or was he still holding a grudge?

Can't hurt to ask, she told herself, pushing the button to dial his number. She held her breath, listening to the ringing on the other end of the line, more relieved than she should have been when he didn't pick up.

She was happy to leave a message on his voice mail. "Hi Raoul, it's Megan O'Ryan. I need your help, please call me when you get a chance, thanks."

"Who's Raoul?" Luke asked from the doorway.

She was proud of herself for not jumping like a scared rabbit, since she'd been engrossed in the phone call and hadn't heard him approach. "Raoul Lee is the chief microbiologist at the Chicago CSI crime lab, and I was hoping to get his help with processing our evidence. Either to have him do the work himself or to pull some strings with the Madison lab."

The furrow between Luke's brows disappeared. "That would be great. I'm afraid the murderer is going to strike again and we don't even have a single clue processed yet."

"Yeah, the first murder happened Friday night, he left the beer bottle in my motel room on Saturday. Makes me wonder if he picked a weekend on purpose, knowing we wouldn't get very far until Monday."

"Possibly," Luke agreed. He watched her for a moment and then said, "I have to head home for a bit, I need to talk to Sam. Is there anything I can get you before I go?"

She was ashamed at how badly she wanted him to stay. But of course he had to check on Sam. His son was going through a tough time, and she knew Luke was worried about him. "No, thanks, I'll be fine. I thought I'd keep reviewing the transcript of Sherman's trial."

He frowned. "I don't want you to read it if it's going to bother you. You need some rest, Megan. Relax and read a book."

The only book she had with her was a murder mystery, and somehow that wasn't appealing at the moment. She'd picked it up at the store last week, not expecting to be thrust into a murder investigation of her own. "I'll be fine, don't worry."

Luke hesitated for a minute, but then nodded. "The dispatcher, or any of the deputies for that matter, can reach me at any time if you need something."

"All right. Tell Sam hi for me."

A ghost of a smile flickered in Luke's eyes. "I will."

When he turned and walked away, it took everything she possessed not to go running after him.

Luke forced himself to leave Megan, even though he didn't want to. She was safe enough here in the building, with the deputies and the dispatcher around.

Frank had told him the interview with Sam hadn't gone well. So no matter how much he wanted to spend time with Megan, his son needed him.

"He wouldn't say much," Frank had said, scratching his jaw. "Confirmed he was the last one to see Liza alive, but that she was fine when he left. Apparently he went back to crash at his friend Doug's house. And he told me he was at a bonfire down at the south shore the night of the motel break-in. He did give me a list of all the kids who were at both parties."

Luke had scanned the list, not too surprised to notice it was basically the same group of kids. Mostly seniors, except for Sam and Doug. "All right, thanks for doing the interview, Frank. What he told you matches what he told me, so hopefully he's telling the truth. But I think we need to continue talking to these kids."

"I'm on it. I've already talked to a couple of them. I'll talk to them again about the second bonfire and get to the kids I missed as well."

Luke trusted Frank would do exactly that. Even though Frank was looking forward to retirement, he wasn't a slouch on the job. Not like some of the younger deputies, who did their best to get by on the bare minimum.

He headed for home, trying to think of a way to get Sam to open up a little. He stopped at the store, picking up a couple of steaks and the fixings for a salad, hoping that sharing dinner together might help reestablish some semblance of a relationship.

His hopeful mood vanished the minute he pulled into the driveway.

Sam's rusted black truck was not parked anywhere in sight. He'd confiscated Sam's keys, but his son could have had a spare hidden.

Although if that was the case, why had he walked to the bonfire on Saturday night? Irritated, he slammed the squad door and carried the groceries into the house.

"Sam? Are you in here?" he called as he headed into the kitchen to set the grocery bags on the table. Why did

Sam keep pulling these kinds of stunts? His son knew very well he was grounded. Hadn't he just been interviewed by a deputy regarding a murder investigation?

What on earth was Sam thinking? Hadn't the seriousness of the situation sunk into his tiny teenage brain?

Muttering under his breath, Luke marched through the house, opening the door to Sam's room without knocking.

The room was glaringly empty. As was the rest of the house. His son wasn't anywhere to be found.

He opened his cell phone and called Sam's number. But of course the ringing on the other end of the line went to voice mail.

Sam didn't pick up.

Snapping his phone shut, he fought a wave of pure helplessness. Sam was gone and he wasn't answering his phone. Did that mean he'd taken off for good? What if Sam was so angry he'd never come back?

Luke sank down onto the sofa and buried his face in his hands, desolation overwhelming him.

He'd failed Sam. Again. There was no denying this mess was his fault as much as Sam's. He'd spent most of the day, on Sunday no less, at work. He was gone all the time. Was it any wonder Sam had taken off? He never should have taken on the added responsibility. He should have told Mayor Ganzer to give the job of interim sheriff to someone else.

Anyone else.

He scrubbed his hands over his face. He was making the same mistakes he'd made back in Milwaukee. Only this time, instead of drowning his sorrows in a bottle, he chose to bury himself in his work.

Either way, the end result was the same. He was losing his son. Had possibly already lost him.

Desperate, he opened his phone and sent a text message. The first one he'd typed was a curt, where are you? But then he erased it and sent a plea instead. *Sam, please come home. I love you and I want you to come home.*

After sending the text message, he stared blindly at his phone, waiting for a response.

But Sam didn't reply.

Was he too late?

Dear Lord, please watch over Sam. Please guide him down the right path. Bring him home to me. And please, please keep him safe from harm. Amen.

NINE

Luke didn't sleep well. Twice he'd gotten up to walk through the house when he'd thought he'd heard sounds indicating Sam had come home.

But Sam hadn't returned. And still wasn't home when Luke gave up trying to sleep at six o'clock in the morning.

After he showered and dressed in his uniform, he decided to drive around looking for Sam's truck. He wasn't sure what Sam's work schedule was at Rose's diner, so he started there.

Sam's truck wasn't parked behind the diner, but Luke didn't let that stop him from going inside. "Hi, Josie. Have you seen Sam this morning?"

"No, Sheriff, but he wasn't scheduled to work today. He is on the schedule again for the early shift tomorrow though."

It was humbling to have to ask others about his son's activities. "Ah, has he been showing up for all his scheduled shifts over the weekend?"

Josie flashed a sympathetic smile, as if she could relate to the trials and tribulations of raising teenagers. "Yes, he did. Sam doesn't call in sick very often. He doesn't say much, but he's a good employee and a hard worker. I don't care what the rest of the town thinks, he's not a bad kid."

Her comments were nice to hear, Even though they only reinforced how it was his relationship with his son that was the problem. And he didn't like hearing that the rest of the townsfolk didn't like his son much. "Thanks, Josie."

"You're welcome, Sheriff. Would you like a cup of coffee on the house?"

"No, thanks." Coffee was tempting, as he was exhausted, but he could get some later. He left the diner and headed back to his squad car. Okay, so maybe Sam hadn't really left town. Could be that he'd overreacted a bit, although Sam had still taken the truck when he was grounded.

Luke drove slowly through town, searching for signs of Sam's truck. When he didn't see it anywhere, he decided to go to Doug's house. Sam's friend's house wasn't far from theirs, just two houses down along the lake.

It was very early to be paying a visit, and his heart sank a bit when he didn't find Sam's truck in Doug's driveway. He was debating whether he should wake up the occupants inside or come back later when a car pulled into the driveway.

A woman he estimated to be in her early forties climbed out of the car. She wore navy blue scrubs and had a heavy black stethoscope draped around her neck. She walked down the driveway toward him, her gaze wary. "Sheriff? Is there something I can do for you?"

"Hi, Ms. Larson, sorry to bother you so early, but I'm looking for my son, Sam. I know he hangs out here a lot."

"No, I haven't seen Sam or Doug for that matter. I've

been working twelve-hour night shifts all weekend. I did talk to Doug on the phone several times, though. I'm sure Doug is still sleeping, but you're welcome to come inside."

He tipped his hat. "Thank you, I'd appreciate that." He followed her inside and stood in the foyer while she went down to her son's room.

When she returned a few minutes later, her gaze was troubled. "Doug isn't here. I know I spoke to him last night around nine o'clock. He didn't tell me he was going anywhere. You say Sam is missing too?"

"Yes, I know Sam was home around five but by the time I got home at seven he was gone. He isn't supposed to be driving his truck. In fact, I took his keys. But he must have had another set, because the truck is gone."

Ms. Larson pursed her lips. "Doug's car is in the garage, so I think we can assume they're together."

For some reason, that idea was reassuring. Maybe Sam hadn't totally skipped town, the way he'd feared. More likely, Sam and Doug had taken off to go somewhere.

But where?

"If you hear from Doug, would you mind calling me?" Luke asked.

"Of course. And let me give you my cell phone number too."

He could have told her that it was highly unlikely he'd hear from Sam before she heard from her son, but he willingly exchanged cell phone numbers anyway. He tucked her number into his breast pocket. "Thanks, Ms. Larson."

"Please, call me Lynette." Her smile was strained.

"I'm sure the boys are fine. We're probably worrying over nothing."

He wished he could believe that, and hated to know that he'd worried her too. Although she would have been concerned anyway when she came home to find Doug was gone. He thanked her and left the house, returning to his squad car. He took a long drive along the lake, but didn't see any sign of Sam's distinctive vehicle.

With a sigh, he turned and headed back into town, toward the sheriff's department headquarters. Once he was in his office, with a large mug of black coffee to help keep the fatigue at bay, he tried again, for what seemed like the hundredth time, to call Sam. And when that didn't work, he sent another text message.

Please call. I'm worried about you. So is Doug's mom. We want to know you're ok.

He set the phone aside, hoping for a response he didn't really expect to get, and tried to bury himself in the investigation of Liza's murder. He wanted to give up his job as interim sheriff, but solving the murder had to take top priority.

Bad enough he was failing as a father; he refused to fail in finding answers for Liza's parents as well.

Megan was scheduled to work in the Madison crime lab on Monday, so she hand-delivered the Point beer bottle that had been left in her motel room on Saturday night. After it was safely logged and tagged, she returned to her space in the lab and tried to focus on her work. Heaven knew there was plenty to keep her busy.

About an hour into her shift, Raoul Lee returned her phone call. "I got your message," he said bluntly.

"Thanks for calling me back," Megan said, infusing warmth into her tone. "How have you been, Raoul?"

"Bryan Cordell is in charge of the micro lab in Madison," Raoul said, brushing past her attempt to be civil. "You can talk to him directly, I've already paved the way for you since he owes me a favor. He'll get your evidence moved to the top of the heap."

She recognized Bryan Cordell's name, of course, considering he was one of the department heads. She was impressed that Raoul knew him well enough to call in a favor, although she suspected Raoul's reputation for being a brilliant scientist probably helped. Raoul had worked in several well-known crime labs before coming to Chicago. All the big centers fought for his expertise.

She'd been lucky to learn from the best of the best.

"Great, thanks for the tip." She didn't report to Bryan but knew how to find him. "I will talk to him if you think it will help. I really appreciate the information."

There was a brief silence on the other end of the line. She was getting the distinct impression that Raoul wasn't very happy with her. "Are you okay, Raoul? Is there something I can do for you? Is something wrong?"

Another long pause. "Nothing is wrong. Do you have time to get together, Megan?" Raoul asked, unexpectedly. "I know you're working in Madison and living in Crystal Lake, but are you coming back to Chicago anytime soon?"

"No, I'm sorry, but I don't have any plans to come back to Chicago anytime soon. And I'm fairly busy at the moment, helping the Madison crime lab get caught up on their DNA testing. I like living in Crystal Lake."

To be honest, she actually liked being around the interim sheriff Luke Torretti. Crystal Lake would be a nice place to live, if not for the murder of a young girl.

A killer who was taunting Megan.

"Fine. I have to go. Call me again when you don't need a favor." Raoul hung up, and there had been no mistaking the annoyance in his tone.

With a wince, she hung up the phone. Her former mentor was not happy with her.

Because she'd only called him when she needed help? Maybe. She stared down at her phone for a long moment. When was the last time she'd kept in touch with her friends? Months. Years. Since the trial. Even before the trial, when she'd buried herself in sorrow and work.

Maybe Raoul was right to be upset with her. Being a friend was a two-way street. She needed to keep in touch with her friends if she wanted them to be there for her.

Vowing to do better, she finished the DNA sample she was working on and then took a break to call Bryan Cordell. Luckily his number was listed in the online staff directory.

He asked her to come to his office, so she walked down the hall to where the management offices were located. The lab didn't have any windows, but the offices lined the outside of the building, and with the doors open she could see outside. She was surprised to discover it was overcast. The sky looked dark and thunderous, as if it were about to rain.

"Come in," Bryan said, greeting her heartily. He was older than she'd anticipated, maybe in his sixties. He gestured to the chair opposite his desk and she sat down.

"Thank you. I'm sure Raoul told you we're working on a brutal murder of a teenage girl in Crystal Lake, Wisconsin. I know your DNA testing is behind, as I've been hired to assist with the backlog, but if there was a way to put Liza Campbell's evidence at the top of the list, I'd appreciate it. We certainly need all the help we can get."

"We? Are you working the case too?" he asked.

"Only in a volunteer capacity." She didn't add that she would have been dragged into the investigation anyway, since the murderer had chosen her backyard as the place to kill his young victim.

"I'm aware of the Liza Campbell case—her autopsy is being performed as we speak. Exactly what evidence do you need rushed?"

It was on the tip of her tongue to say all of it. She thought back to the clues they'd collected so far and what, in her opinion, should be top priority. "We'd like to match the thread found at the suspected scene of the crime to the fabric of her shorts," she said. "We'd also like to match up the soil samples from that same area to what was embedded in the heel of her shoe, if possible. I'd like to know if there are any particles embedded in the braided rope, either from a specific type of glove or maybe skin cells. And I brought in a Point beer bottle that we suspect is the bottle that Liza was drinking from, but we need that verified as well."

"Hmm. The thread and soil won't be an issue, we can complete that readily enough. The rope will take some time, but I could put someone on that too. The DNA testing on the bottle might be a problem," he mused slowly. "We're getting pressure from the governor to get the oldest samples done first, before adding new ones."

"I understand, sir. But we might be dealing with a copycat murderer. There are some similarities between Liza's murder and Paul Sherman's victims. Since he's still in jail, serving three consecutive life sentences, we have to assume someone is copying his M.O. The sooner we have something to go on, the more likely we can avoid more victims."

Bryan stared at her thoughtfully for a moment and then nodded. "All right, you've convinced me. I'll move the beer bottle to the top of the DNA list."

"Thank you, sir." She gave him the ID number of the evidence she'd turned in that morning, and then rose to her feet. "I appreciate your help on this."

"Ms. O'Ryan?" he called, when she'd reached the doorway.

"Yes?" she turned back around to face him.

"I understand you're a temporary employee here, correct?" She nodded and he continued, "After Raoul called, I looked you up. Your credentials are impressive. If you're interested in a permanent position here in the lab, let me know."

She didn't bother to hide her surprise. "Thanks, sir, I will."

After leaving Bryan's office she returned to her corner of the lab and began to work in earnest. DNA testing couldn't be rushed; however, she could work through her lunch if necessary.

She did take a few seconds to call Luke but was sent straight to his voice mail. She left him a message about Liza's autopsy and the evidence that would hopefully be processed by the end of the day.

As she worked, she kept an eye on her phone, wishing Luke would return her call. And she couldn't help but wonder, what would Luke think if she accepted a permanent full-time position in Madison?

"Megan, time to clock out," Sharon said from behind her, pulling her attention away from the DNA sample she'd almost finished.

Surprised, she glanced up at the clock. It was later than she'd realized. "I'll have this sample finished in twenty minutes."

Sharon frowned. "I don't know, we're not supposed to allow employees to work overtime."

It was one of the most frustrating things about working for the state government. They had a tremendous backlog of DNA samples yet they were bound by budget constraints and wouldn't approve overtime to get the job done. "I'm only part-time, and a temporary position at that. I'm not even scheduled to work tomorrow. Surely another twenty minutes won't matter."

Her supervisor hesitated, then granted her permission with a nod. "You're right. Go ahead and finish what you're working on."

"Thanks." Glancing around, she noticed the lab was pretty much deserted. The other technologists must have left at five o'clock on the dot.

As she finished up her sample, she wondered about Liza's evidence. Bryan had moved them to the top of the list, but she hadn't heard anything about the results. Had they finished them? Had they sent them directly to the sheriff's department?

Luke hadn't returned her phone call and she tried not

to take that personally. Obviously he was busy, between his sheriff's duties and his son. He wasn't avoiding her.

Was he?

She clocked out at five-thirty and made her way outside. The moment she opened the door, she stepped into a deluge of rain.

Ducking her head, she dashed across the basically deserted parking lot to her car. The storm clouds stretched across the sky made it seem later than five-thirty in the evening.

With her windshield wipers on high, she slowly headed onto the interstate. The traffic was light, thankfully. But she quickly noticed the dark green car that kept pace behind her.

She frowned, staring at her rearview mirror. Was the car really following her? Or was this another instance where her paranoia was getting the better of her? She drove past an exit ramp, and the green car stayed roughly two car lengths behind her.

The message written on her bathroom mirror hadn't been her imagination. Nor had the break-in to her motel room.

She switched lanes and the green car did the same less than a minute later. She took her foot off the gas pedal, encouraging the car to come closer so she could memorize the license-plate number.

Despite the hazards of talking on the phone while driving in the rain, she flipped open her cell phone and called Luke. She quickly slipped on the ear piece.

This time, he picked up the call. "Hi, Megan. I got your message, thanks. Today we have a lot of good news. We've verified that Sean Mathews is in the army, so he's off our suspect list. The test results on Liza's autopsy, the thread we found and the soil have all come in. They're a match. We've confirmed she was murdered outside your house."

"That's great, Luke," she said, truly glad to hear the news.

"The contents of the Point beer bottle revealed traces of Rohypnol in the contents, and they're checking the tox screen on Liza's blood to see if the drug is in her system as well."

"Really?" For a moment she was distracted from the green car steadily following her. "Paul Sherman used drugs to subdue his victims. Another similarity in the killer's M.O."

"Yeah, although he wasn't always consistent. He used ether on a couple of women, instead of putting the drug in their drinks."

She tightened her grip on the steering wheel. Yes, she was very familiar with how Sherman subdued his victims. Katie's autopsy had showed she had Rohypnol in her bloodstream. "I know, but you'll find that in my sister's case, she was given Rohypnol just like Liza was. It could be that Sherman couldn't get anymore ether after the first two victims. Or it could be a matter of how he stalked his victims. Maybe he learned that following them for a while, meeting them first in some bar, added to the thrill of the crime."

"Could be," Luke agreed.

A horrible thought struck. "Luke, what if the copycat killer is re-creating all of Sherman's crimes? Sherman's last victim had Rohypnol in her drug screen, and so this killer has done the same with Liza? Maybe he plans to re-create the other two victims as well?"

There was a long silence on the other end of the line

as Luke digested her theory. "Well, if he is a copycat killer, he will strike again."

"I know." She hesitated and glanced in the rearview mirror again. "Would you do me a favor? There's a car that seems to be following me, the license plate number is RFL 994. Would you run it through the DMV system?"

"What? Where are you?" Luke demanded. She could hear the tapping of the keyboard as he brought up the DMV system. "You should have said something right away. I'll have a squad car meet you."

"I'm about fifteen miles from Crystal Lake, just past Lyon Road, exit two-thirty-two." She strove to hide her nervousness. "It's pouring like crazy, so he could be driving behind me to follow my taillights." It was the only explanation she could come up with. In her experience, people tended to pass each other on the highway, not keep a consistent pace behind them.

Of course, if he was following her, he wasn't trying very hard to hide the fact.

The thought made her relax a bit.

"Okay, the car is registered to a Willie Johannes, he's a seventy-two-year-old man, five foot eleven inches and two hundred and fifty pounds."

Not a guy who would likely be following her. Even as she watched, the car dropped back a few feet. "Is there anything you can find out about Willie? Like where he lives? Maybe he lives near Crystal Lake and this is all just a big coincidence."

"Hang on a minute," Luke muttered. She could hear the keyboard tapping again. "I sent a deputy out to meet you, so help is on the way. I'll look up our friend Willie."

Just talking to Luke made her feel calmer. Not just because he was the sheriff in charge of a murder investigation, although that certainly helped. But her feelings were for the man, not the office.

Jake had been a cop too, but he hadn't inspired the same confidence. The same sense of safeness. The reassurance of being protected.

No, in fact, just the opposite. She'd always been on edge around Jake. His unpredictable nature had made her nervous. She'd never been sure what to expect with Jake. One minute he was happy-go-lucky, the next he was surly.

Luke seemed to be there for her, no matter what. Hard to believe she'd only known him for a few days.

She glanced again in the rearview mirror, perturbed to note the green car had closed the gap between them. Did the guy know she was on the phone with the authorities? Was he sensing she was trying to get away?

Despite the rain, she stepped a little harder on the gas pedal.

"Megan? I want you to take the next exit, which is Highway ZZ, okay?" There was obvious tension in Luke's tone. "Don't use your blinker, just get off the highway at the very last moment. I want you to put as much distance as you can between you and the guy following you."

"Why?" She passed a sign that claimed Hwy ZZ was two miles ahead. Two miles that would seem like twenty. "What have you found out?"

"Willie Johannes, whose last known address was just outside of Madison, died two years ago. We don't know who is driving the car behind you, and it could be our killer."

TEN

Megan gripped the steering wheel tightly as she peered through the rain, trying to gauge the distance to the exit. One hundred feet, fifty feet, twenty feet, ten feet, *now!*

She yanked the steering wheel to the right, her stomach clenching in fear when the rear end of her car fishtailed on the slick pavement. She managed to bring the car back under control, barely noticing the way her cell phone sailed across the car from the passenger seat, landing somewhere on the floor, breaking her connection with Luke.

As she approached the stop sign at the bottom of the exit ramp, she risked a glance in the rearview mirror. Horrified, she watched as the green car clipped the edge of the guard rail, jumping the edge of the ramp to follow her off the interstate.

Her heart dropped to the bottom of her stomach. There was no mistaking the driver's intent.

Liza's killer was coming after her!

The driver of the green car closed the gap quickly, and just as she reached the stop sign, he rammed into her car from behind. Her little Sunfire spun crazily on the slick road and skidded right toward the deep culvert lining the road.

She wrenched the steering wheel at the last minute, in an attempt to save her car engine. She slid sideways, her passenger side taking the brunt of the damage as she hit the bottom of the culvert with a bone-jarring thud. Frantically, she pulled on the door handle, thankful to have the strength to raise the driver's side door. In the distance she could hear the faint wail of police sirens.

Too far away. The sheriff's deputy would never get here in time.

She crawled out of the car and scrambled up the edge of the ditch using her hands to grab weeds and brush to help keep her balance. Her low-heeled shoes sank into the mud, so she kicked them off. From somewhere behind her, she heard the soft snick of a car door shutting.

No! He was coming after her!

Brushing the rain from her eyes, she desperately surveyed the landscape and considered her options as she ran. She needed shelter. A place to hide. There were some trees about a hundred feet from the edge of the road, but to reach them she'd be in full view.

Regardless, she headed in that direction.

Please Lord, save me!

She ran as fast as she could in her bare feet, fully expecting the sound of gunfire. Or to be grabbed roughly from behind, a braided rope tossed around her neck. The wailing sirens grew louder and louder.

Help was on the way. She only needed to hang on for a few minutes longer.

She reached the grove of trees and kept going, weaving among the towering tree trunks, the leaves overhead cutting down the force of the rain. She was soaked to the skin, shivering as she stumbled over roots and pushed away tree branches that slapped her in the face. Finally she stopped, hanging on to a tree trunk and breathing heavily.

She glanced at the spot where her car had gone into the ditch. There was no sign of the green car. Not parked on the road or anywhere on the highway going in either direction as far as she could see.

He was gone.

She closed her eyes and rested her forehead against the smooth bark.

Thank You, Lord. Thank You for protecting me.

She remained in her hiding place until the deputy's squad car pulled over to the side of the road, right next to her slightly crumpled car. Then, releasing her grip on the tree trunk, she hobbled across the grassy terrain, back toward the edge of the road lined by the ditch. The deputy was shining his flashlight inside her car.

"Here!" she called out hoarsely. "I'm here!"

"Ms. O'Ryan?" The flashlight swung in her direction and she lifted her arm to shield her eyes from the bright light. "Are you all right, ma'am?"

She nodded as she came closer. She was never so happy to see anyone in her entire life. She stood, wrapping her arms around her waist to keep steady. "The man in the green car rammed into me, sending me into the ditch. I ran for shelter, because I heard him coming after me."

The deputy was a younger man she didn't recognize, but he was kind as he looked at her with sympathy. "It's okay, ma'am. You're safe now. I'll get a tow truck for your car." He opened the trunk of his car, pulled out a blanket and then helped her inside the back of the squad car. "Here, wrap up in this."

She clutched the blanket around her shoulders and sank into the cushioned car seat gratefully. Her feet were covered in mud and hurt from the scratches she'd sustained, but overall, she was deeply humbled at how she'd managed to escape serious harm.

God had watched over her and Luke sent help.

At the sheriff's department headquarters, Luke met them outside the moment Deputy Scott drove up. Without a word Luke helped her from the car, noticed her bare feet and then swept her into his arms to carry her inside.

She rested her head on his shoulder gratefully. Inside the building, he hesitated and tightened his arms as if he didn't want to let her go.

"I'm fine," she murmured reassuringly. As much as she would have preferred to stay in his arms, she knew that wasn't exactly a viable option. The dispatcher, a woman whose name escaped her at the moment, watched them curiously.

He finally strode into his office and set her down in the chair tucked into the corner. "Wait here," he said before he disappeared into the main room.

Within moments, Luke returned carrying a mug of hot coffee. She wrapped her hands around the mug for warmth and sipped the brew gratefully. He disappeared again, this time returning with a bucket of warm, sudsy water and a towel.

He knelt beside her and gently lifted one foot and then the other, placing them in the warm soapy water.

She sucked in a quick breath at the stinging pain from

the various cuts. But she didn't cry out or move her feet. The deep scratches needed to be cleaned out.

She was lucky, very lucky she wasn't hurt worse.

"I'm so glad you're all right," Luke murmured, still on his knees in front of her. "I almost lost my mind when our phone connection was cut off."

"I'm sorry." She reached out and gently stroked his cheek. For a moment they simply stared at each other. Then Luke slowly drew away, rising to his feet.

The concerned man was quickly replaced by the hard-edged cop. "Tell me again exactly what happened," Luke commanded.

She did as he asked. "He followed me off the exit ramp and then rammed his car into mine. I slid sideways into the ditch, but managed to climb out of the car. I heard him come after me as I was crawling out of the ditch." The memories were far too vivid, and her voice dropped lower. "If you hadn't already sent a deputy, he might have caught me."

Luke's expression turned grim. "Megan, I think we have to assume this guy killed Liza and has now decided to come after you. He's not just leaving clues anymore, taunting you. He could have killed you tonight."

She nodded helplessly. Hadn't she thought the same thing? "It doesn't make sense, though. Why bother to copy Sherman's M.O. for just one murder? Unless…" Her voice trailed off, hardly able to voice the horrible thought.

"Unless what?" Luke asked.

Dear God, no. Oh, no. She hoped, prayed she was wrong. But if she wasn't? "Unless—he's already killed another girl and we haven't found the body yet."

* * *

Luke didn't even want to consider the possibility of another victim. Up until this point, he'd been distracted by the killer's games, his way of leaving clues around Megan.

What if that was the killer's intent? To keep him focused on the wrong thing?

He'd spent hours on the case, comparing notes from Liza's death to the St. Patrick's Strangler, but so far he hadn't come up with much. Until today, when some of his earlier theories had been proven correct.

"You could be right," he finally agreed. "But so far we've done our best to send out warning messages to all young women, asking them to be careful. They've been instructed to always go out in pairs. I have to believe if a girl went missing, we'd have heard about it."

Although look how long Sam and Doug had been missing, and he certainly hadn't filed a missing person's report. Was it possible someone else was gone and the alarm simply hadn't been sounded yet?

"I hope you're right," Megan murmured. With her auburn hair plastered to her head, she looked all of fifteen, even though he knew very well from running the DMV check on her that very first day that she was almost thirty. Too old to match the killer's M.O.

Which didn't seem to matter, since there was no doubt in his mind that the killer had gone after her this evening.

A low rumble reached his ears, and when Megan's cheeks turned pink he realized the sound had come from her. Her stomach was growling with hunger.

"How about if I take you to my house for a bit?" he asked, changing the subject. Megan deserved a break after everything she'd been through. "You can shower and change into dry clothes while I cook us dinner."

The way her eyes brightened at the offer, he could tell she was tempted by the idea. "You cook?" she asked skeptically.

He chuckled. "How could I not? After I managed to pull myself together after my wife died, I took a crash course in making meals. Nothing fancy, mind you, but I can hold my own. It just so happens I have a few steaks in the fridge and fresh fixings for a salad." The meal he'd hoped to make for Sam. He frowned and quirked a brow. "Please tell me you're not a vegetarian?"

She laughed, a low husky sound that curled around his heart. "No, I'm not a vegetarian. Steak and salad actually sounds wonderful."

When she lifted her feet out of the soapy water, he saw the extent of the cuts and grimaced. "Do you happen to have a spare set of shoes?" he asked doubtfully. Not that he minded carrying her.

In fact, he rather preferred it.

"Yes, I have a pair of running shoes and socks under the cot next to my suitcase."

He stifled the flash of disappointment and went to fetch them for her. She kept the blanket wrapped around her shoulders as she tentatively walked down the hall to gather some clean clothes.

The rain had subsided to nothing more than an annoying drizzle. As he drove to his house, the first thing he looked for was Sam's familiar truck.

The knot in his gut twisted when there was no sign of his son. He checked his cell phone again, but there was no response to his numerous text messages. Or anything from Lynette, Doug's mother, indicating she'd heard from the boys.

Where could Sam be?

"Help yourself to the bathroom facilities," he said, heading for the kitchen to pull food from the refrigerator. "I'll have dinner ready by the time you're finished."

"Thanks, Luke." She flashed him a grateful smile before heading down the hall toward the bathroom.

He took his time making the salad and then carried the steaks outside to the grill. Luckily his gas grill was protected from the rain by the overhang of the house, so he put the steaks on and then stood with his back propped against the wall, gazing out at the lake.

The rain had put a severe dent in the boating fun. The lake was pretty much deserted except for a lone fisherman, sitting on a boat in the middle of the lake, who didn't seem to mind getting wet.

He flipped the steaks, trying to take advantage of the peaceful atmosphere. But he was all too aware that a killer who'd tried to hurt Megan tonight was still out there, somewhere.

The APB had gone out for the green car almost instantly. But so far, they hadn't found it. One of the downfalls of living way out in the country was that there were too many winding highways and roads to keep a close eye on all of them. With only four deputies on in the evenings, and three on overnight, it could take hours to find the vehicle.

Megan's car had been towed to a local garage and the guy in charge had agreed to look at it first thing in the morning.

He carried the steaks back into the house, surprised

to find Megan wearing a long-sleeved shirt and jeans, seated at his kitchen table talking on her cell phone. He blatantly eavesdropped on her side of the conversation, setting the plate on the counter and turning to face her.

"Thanks for checking into this for me, Michael," she said. "And please let me know if you find anything."

After she snapped her cell phone shut, she glanced up at him, answering the unspoken question in his eyes. "That was my former CSI partner, Michael Bennett. We worked together for over four years. I asked him to check on Jake, see if he did actually go back to Chicago the way he claimed."

He didn't bother to hide his shock. "You think he was the driver of the green car? Did you get a good look at him?"

She blew out a breath. "No, I didn't get a good look at him. And I don't really know what to believe. I guess I just wanted to make sure that Jake was back in Chicago."

Odd that she hadn't said anything to him about her concerns. "Is there a reason you don't trust me to check on Feeney?" he asked slowly.

"No, of course not. Please don't think that." She paused and then added, "I knew you'd probably check up on Jake yourself, and I wasn't sure if you'd get cooperation from the Chicago P.D. So I asked Michael for a favor. He'll have connections within the police department that you won't have. You should know Michael never thought very highly of Jake."

A sentiment he could certainly agree with. Obviously, he and this Michael guy would get along great. Except he didn't know what to make of her relationship with her former partner. Were they friends? Obviously. More than friends? He wanted to ask but knew he would only sound jealous.

Megan was here with him now. Not with Michael Bennett. And that was all that mattered. Besides, they were smack in the middle of a murder investigation. This wasn't the time to be thinking of his personal life.

Or lack thereof.

He brought over the steaks and salads and after a quick murmured prayer, there was a companionable silence as they ate their meal.

"Everything is delicious, Luke. Thanks for inviting me," she said, taking a sip of her water.

"You're more than welcome." He smiled at her, thinking she looked right at home seated at his kitchen table. "I should thank you, because otherwise I'd be eating all alone."

"Where is Sam?" she asked.

His appetite vanished as he let out a heavy sigh. "I wish I knew. I haven't seen him since late yesterday afternoon. I looked all over for him, but so far haven't found him. His friend Doug seems to be missing as well, so it's logical to assume they're out doing something together."

Hopefully nothing illegal. He'd brought Sam to Crystal Lake to avoid his getting involved in criminal activity. But now Sam was drinking. And who knew what else.

Megan reached over to put her hand on his arm, a gesture of comfort. "I'm sorry, Luke. I can only imagine what you've been going through."

The fact that she felt bad for him, when she was the one who was rammed into a ditch and forced to run for her life, humbled him. Had he ever met anyone like her? Megan O'Ryan was a truly amazing woman. "Thanks, but you've been through much worse tonight. Sam is seventeen and more than capable of taking care of himself."

She frowned. "Maybe, although I used to think I was, too."

She was right. The karate lessons Sam had taken as a youngster wouldn't help against a knife or a bullet.

"Sorry," she said again, reading the expression on his face. "I didn't mean to worry you again. I'm sure he's fine."

He wasn't sure how to tell her he was worried about what Sam might be doing, as well as worried about any physical danger he might run into. "I'm sure he is fine. I can't help being angry with him, though. It's extremely irresponsible of him to take off without telling anyone where he went. Doug's mother is divorced and working night shifts at the Hope County Hospital. She's worried, too. I'm afraid my son is a bad influence on his friends."

She tightened her hand on his arm. "Luke, I highly doubt Doug was dragged along with Sam, kicking and screaming in protest," she said drily. "At this point, they're both being irresponsible."

That much was true. But he knew the real reason Sam had disappeared. "I asked Frank to interview Sam, because he was the last one to see Liza the night she died. And he didn't have an alibi for the time frame of the murder, or for the time frame of the break-in at the motel," he confessed. "I think Sam took off after that, because he was angry with me. But I had to do it. I can't protect him too much. This is a murder investigation. I already covered for him as long as I could."

"I know," she murmured, her wide green eyes full of sympathy. "He's too young to really understand the impact of his actions."

Not that young. But Sam often jumped to conclusions rather than giving his father the benefit of the doubt.

He stared at her hand, noting the angry red scratches that marred her skin. Just another reminder of how close he'd come to losing her. He was lucky to have her here, as support. He reached over and covered her hand with his. "Megan," he began, and then cut himself off.

What was he thinking, turning this moment personal? She needed a friend right now.

Nothing more.

Resolutely, he removed his hand and pulled out from her grasp. He rose to his feet, carrying his plate and salad bowl over to the sink.

Distance. He gripped the edge of the sink, taking a deep breath. He needed distance to stop himself from doing something he'd regret.

"Luke?" Megan came over to stand beside him, placing her empty dishes on the counter. She was so close, he could almost feel her brushing against him. "Did I say something wrong?"

Her scent, fresh from the shower, filled his head. "No, Megan." His voice was too low and husky so he tried again, concentrating on the task of rinsing the dishes. "It's getting late, I need to drive you back to headquarters. Sit down and relax, this will only take a minute."

"I should wash up, since you cooked," she protested, moving in closer, trying to take the scrub brush out of his hand.

He wasn't sure what happened, but one moment they were playing tug-of-war with the scrub brush and the next she was in his arms.

For a long moment he simply held her close. But she lifted her head to stare up at him. He pulled away enough to look down at her.

"Megan," he whispered, brushing her hair away from her face and tipping her chin up with his finger, so he could look into her eyes. "I care about you. A lot. Please tell me if you want me to stop."

She held his gaze and slowly shook her head. "I don't want you to stop."

He lowered his head and kissed her. Her mouth was sweet. Soft. Enticing. The kiss opened up a heart he thought was long dead, swelling with an emotion he dared not name.

"Dad?"

Luke jerked his head up and broke away from Megan, slamming his hip sharply against the edge of the counter. He ignored the sharp pain, hardly able to believe his eyes as he gaped at Sam, who stared at them incredulously.

ELEVEN

Luke tried to pull his scattered thoughts together. His first instinct was to yell at Sam and demand to know where he'd been. But he wrestled his annoyance under control, knowing that yelling at his son would only push Sam further away.

The irony of the role reversal didn't escape his notice. Shouldn't he be the one walking in on his son kissing a girl? He glanced at Megan, whose pink cheeks betrayed her acute embarrassment.

"Excuse me," she said, glancing between them both. "I'll, ah, leave you alone." She quickly escaped down the hall to the bathroom, giving him and Sam some much-needed privacy.

Luke cleared his throat. "Sam, I'm glad you're home."

"Yeah. I can tell you really missed me." Sam's sarcasm made him wince.

"Actually, I spent most of the day looking for you, had a long conversation with Doug's mother as well," he corrected evenly. "Which reminds me, did Doug go home too? Because his mother was worried."

"Yeah, he's driving my truck since he blew out a tire on his car. He dropped me off and went home."

Which explained why he hadn't heard Sam's truck

pull into the driveway. "You know you're grounded. I wasn't happy to see you'd left without saying a word. Where did you and Doug go?" he asked.

Sam lifted a shoulder. "Nowhere special," he said evasively.

Luke could feel his temper rising. "Sam, I asked you a direct question and I expect an honest answer."

"What difference does it make?" Sam challenged. "You won't believe me no matter what I say."

Beneath the rude and challenging tone he could hear the pain of betrayal. So this was about being questioned by Frank. "That's not true, Sam. I want to trust you, but you're not making it easy, especially when you keep breaking the rules." He kept his tone calm with an effort. He longed to shake some sense into his stubborn son. "If want to know the truth, I asked Frank to interview you because I trust Frank to be fair and honest. I didn't want it to look as if I was protecting you by conducting the interview myself."

Sam stared at him for several long moments. "Why interview me at all? Is everybody in town a suspect?"

"Everyone who doesn't have an alibi for the time frame of the murder," he responded evenly. "And let's face it, son, not only were you the last person to see her alive, but we're still considered outsiders here. When it comes right down to it, the locals are going to point the finger away from anyone who was born and raised in Crystal Lake."

"Yeah, whatever." Was there a hint of understanding in Sam's eyes? Or was that just wishful thinking?

"So where were you?"

There was a long pause. "We decided to do a little camping, out by the deserted farm," Sam reluctantly admitted. "You know, where that big red barn is off Highway JJ? I just needed to get away from everything for a while."

Luke stared at Sam, hoping, praying his son was telling him the truth. "You should have told me and Doug's mom where you were," he insisted.

"Sorry." Sam glanced at the dirty dishes on the counter, the evidence of the cozy meal. "Guess you wish I would have stayed away longer, huh?"

"No, of course not," Megan said briskly, coming back into the room. "Sam, this is your home. Your father was just being nice to me since I was run off the road earlier this evening."

Sam's eyes widened in surprise, both by Megan including herself in the conversation and by her revelation. "Ran off the road? You mean on purpose?"

"Yes, but we don't know who the driver was," Luke was quick to answer. "But that was another reason I was worried about you. There is a killer out there, and just because his first target happened to be a young girl doesn't mean you're safe. No one around here is safe until we get this guy into custody."

"All right, next time I'll let you know where I am," Sam slowly agreed. "The reason you didn't hear from us is because we left without taking our cell-phone chargers. Both our phone batteries went dead."

He wanted to give Sam another lecture on being irresponsible, but decided—since they'd managed to have a relatively nonconfrontational conversation—to leave well enough alone.

"Well, all that matters now is that you're home, safe and sound," Megan said quietly, mirroring his thoughts.

Sam glanced at her warily, as if not sure whether to believe she was sincere or not.

"Sam, I need to take Megan back to the sheriff's department. Are you hungry? There's a leftover steak you could throw on the grill."

"Yeah, I could eat," Sam murmured.

Megan had gathered all her things together, but Luke was reluctant to leave. Seemed like every time he left, Sam pulled a disappearing act. But he couldn't ask Megan to go by herself, especially when she didn't have a car. "Sam —will you be here when I get back?" he hesitantly asked.

Sam hunched his shoulders and nodded. "It's not like I can go anywhere, Doug has my truck."

"All right," Luke said, feeling slightly better, "I'll see you in less than twenty minutes. Okay?"

Sam nodded and crossed over to the fridge to pull out the steak.

"Bye, Sam," Megan said, touching his son's arm with an ease he envied. "Take care."

"You too," Sam murmured, surprising Luke by smiling at Megan.

He tried not to gape at Sam like a hooked fish. When was the last time he'd seen his son smile? Luke could barely remember.

Luke scooped up his keys from the table, following Megan outside. Neither one of them said anything, as they climbed into the squad car.

"I'm sorry if you were embarrassed by Sam walking in on us," Luke said finally breaking the silence.

"Don't worry about it," she said quickly. "I'm just so glad Sam's home. What a relief to know he's safe. I'm sure that has to be a load of worry off your shoulders."

"Yeah." He wasn't sure how to turn the conversation back to the kiss they'd shared in the kitchen without being blunt. Was she upset with him for crossing the line? She'd kissed him back, so he couldn't be sure.

He kept his turbulent thoughts to himself. The drive back to headquarters didn't take long.

He escorted Megan inside, nodding at Walter Grogan, the oldest dispatcher they had in the department. Walter was well past the age of retirement, but insisted he would work until he couldn't. Luke made the introductions. "Walt, this is Megan O'Ryan. Megan, Walter Grogan."

Walt gave a brief nod. "Heard you were staying in the back office," he said gruffly.

"Just for a while," she admitted.

"Keep an eye on her, okay, Walt?" Luke asked.

"'Course I will."

Luke walked Megan down to the office she was using as sleeping quarters. "Anything I can get for you?" he asked, pausing in the doorway.

"No, thanks. I'm fine." She smiled at him. "Go home to your son, Luke."

He hesitated, wishing he dared kiss her again, but the moment had long passed. "Sleep well, Megan," he murmured, before turning to walk away with the intent of taking her advice.

Returning home to mend his relationship with his son, if possible.

Megan stretched out on the cot and then stared blindly at the ceiling, unable to sleep. Every time she closed her eyes, the images of the night flashed through her mind like a preview of a movie.

The car ramming into her. The crazy spin on the slick roads as her car slid sideways into the ditch. The unmistakable sound of a car door closing. Her frantic scramble for shelter.

Her whispered prayer for safety.

The wails of sirens as Deputy Scott came to her rescue.

She was safe. There was no reason to keep ruminating on the series of events. She needed to figure out a way to erase the memories from her mind.

Would God help? Maybe. She couldn't deny that she'd reached out for Him when she feared for her life.

What could it hurt? She closed her eyes and tried to pray.

Help me find peace, Lord. And give us the strength and wisdom to find Liza's killer before anyone else gets hurt. Amen.

She felt better afterward, but somehow sleep continued to elude her, so she got up from her cot and turned the office light back on. With a sigh, she pulled the files for the Sherman murders toward her.

If she couldn't sleep, then she would work. She'd asked for God's help, and maybe this was his way of answering her plea. She couldn't help but think there had to be a clue in here, somewhere. If they were dealing with a copycat murderer, and it seemed likely they were, then the clue might be in the details of the investigation from the previous murders.

Liza had been given Rohypnol, just like Katie. And Liza fought her murderer like Katie had. But Katie had scraped her nails down Sherman's skin, helping them to get a DNA match.

It had been fate, or maybe God's will, when they'd

found a DNA match in the system. Paul Sherman's criminal record, from the aggravated assault when he'd been sixteen, had resulted in a match with the DNA discovered at the crime scene.

Matching Sherman's DNA to the skin found under Katie's nails had sealed his fate. Now he was in jail, where he'd never assault or murder anyone again.

She reviewed the facts of Liza's murder. There was evidence that Liza had struggled, the soil in the heels of her shoes confirmed that. But Liza hadn't gotten DNA evidence from her assailant.

And even if she had, there was no guarantee the killer already had DNA on file.

Megan went back over the first two murder victims. The M.O. on those two were almost exactly the same. Both girls had been subdued by a compound resembling ether. There had been traces of the drug on their lips and on their skin. In the rope around their necks they'd found traces of plastic from what they thought were plastic gloves worn by the killer. Both girls had been found outside the Irish pubs. But they'd never known for sure if the victims had actually been killed there or somewhere else. They'd found no evidence one way or the other.

The crime scenes had been almost too clean.

The detail nagged at her. Why had Sherman changed his M.O. for Katie? Maybe Katie had been more of an impulse killing. The patrons of the pub had confirmed Sherman had been inside, talking to Katie. No one had heard them arguing, and she'd always wondered what had transpired between the two of them.

Had Katie turned down his advances? Was that why

he'd slipped her the drug and then waited for her outside the bar at closing time?

With a frown, she went back to Katie's autopsy. Particles of latex had been found in the rope around her neck. There had been evidence that Katie had been murdered right there on the asphalt parking lot. Small bits of asphalt had been found imbedded in the back of her scalp.

Likely a simple miscalculation on Sherman's part as to how much of the drug she'd ingested.

Maybe in the first two cases, he'd come back to kill the girls at a later date. And with Katie, he hadn't wanted to wait.

So how did that tie into Liza's murder?

She stared at the results until her vision blurred. With tears. With fatigue. With a suffocating sense of loss.

She closed her eyes and tried to get a grip on her emotions.

Katie was gone. No matter how much she wished she could go back and change what had happened. The goal now was to find Liza's murderer and to prevent any more girls from becoming victims.

Including herself.

The next morning, Megan didn't feel nearly as exhausted as she'd anticipated. When she'd finally crawled back into her cot, she'd fallen soundly asleep.

God answering her prayers? Maybe.

She washed up in the tiny bathroom the best she could, swiped a brush through her shoulder-length hair and then ventured out to the main area of the department. Luke was already standing there, impressive in his freshly pressed uniform. Did he get his shirts done at the dry cleaners? Or iron them himself?

For some reason, the image of Luke wielding an iron made her want to smile.

"Hi, Megan." The warmth in his eyes caught her a little off-guard. "How did you sleep?"

"Pretty good, thanks. Any news?" she asked, even though she knew it wasn't likely.

"Your car is being looked at first thing this morning. Apparently they don't think the damage is as bad as they originally thought," he responded.

"That's good to hear."

"They're going to drop it off here later today, but in the meantime, I have an idea I'd like to run past you."

She was surprised, but nodded and followed him into his office. She sat in the chair across from his desk, watching him expectantly.

"What do you think about going with me to the Illinois state prison to talk to Sherman?" he asked.

Her mouth dropped open in surprise. She'd considered the same thing herself, after going through the minor details differences between the victims. "There's no guarantee he'll talk to us," she warned.

"I know. But what else do we have to go on? At the very least we could see if either Kyle Sherman or Everett Dobrowski has been in to see him."

"What do we know about them?" Megan asked.

"Kyle Sherman lives outside of Rockford, Illinois. He works as a security guard. Everett Dobrowski lives in Minneapolis. He's in college there. Neither one have criminal records on file, other than minor traffic citations. We're still working on verifying both of their alibis during the time frame of Liza's murder."

She nodded slowly. So far, neither one of the potential links to Sherman seemed like viable possibilities. But knowing Luke, he would follow through on every detail, no matter what.

"If facing Paul Sherman is too difficult for you, then I'll go alone," Luke said.

She forced a smile and shook her head. "I'm fine. I'm also off work today, so I wouldn't mind taking a road trip to the prison."

"Are you sure?" His gaze searched hers for a moment. "We'll grab something to eat on the way if you don't mind. It's a long drive."

Megan tried not to imagine what it would be like to see her sister's murderer again. She'd faced Paul Sherman with his cold eyes at the trial, of course, but hadn't anticipated ever having to see him again.

Her stomach twisted painfully. She took a deep breath and let it out slowly. She could do this.

Lord, give me strength.

After a quick breakfast from a drive-through fast-food restaurant on the highway, they were on their way.

"How are things with Sam?" she asked, changing the subject from the murders to his son. "Was he home last night when you got there?"

Luke nodded. "Yeah, he was home. Things seem to be okay, at least for the moment. He had to work today, so that should keep him out of trouble for a few hours."

"He's not a bad kid, Luke," she murmured. "I was wrong in my first impression of him."

Luke grimaced and shrugged. "Maybe not that bad, but remember he was drinking the night of Liza's murder. And was the last person to see her alive. I can't help but worry about him."

"True, but I guess what I meant was that deep down, Sam's a good person. I've been around a lot of twisted criminals, and Sam is far from that. He was shocked when he heard I was run off the road. He cares about what happens to people."

Luke nodded. "Yeah, that's what I think too. But I'm glad to hear you confirm my opinion. I'm afraid that my viewpoint is a bit skewed. I don't want to think the worst of Sam, either."

She longed to touch him, to place her hand on his arm reassuringly. "Don't worry, we'll get through this. I believe we're going to find this guy."

He glanced at her in surprise. "That sounds suspiciously like faith."

She blushed and looked up at him. "It is. I've been thinking about faith a lot lately. Ever since attending church on Sunday. Last night, when I was run off the road, I prayed to God for protection. He answered my prayers."

Luke's smile warmed her toes. "I'm glad to hear that. Believe me, I was praying for him to keep you safe, too."

"And then again, last night, I prayed for help in finding Liza's killer," she said. "I have to believe God is going to show us the way."

"I know He will."

Gladness overwhelmed her when he reached over to entwine his fingers around hers.

Feeling at peace for the first time in a very long time, she held his hand all the way to the Illinois state prison.

Luke shut off the car and turned to face her. "Are you ready?"

"As ready as I'll ever be," she admitted. Her stomach was a mass of knots, but she knew that Sherman couldn't hurt her. Or anyone else. Not anymore.

As they walked inside the prison, she couldn't help looking around curiously. She'd never been inside a prison before. Luke had called ahead, so the prison staff were expecting them.

They had to go through a metal detector and a search prior to gaining entrance to the building.

Finally they were led to the main desk. "You'll need to sign the visitor logbook, Sheriff," the guard instructed. "You're the second visitor for this inmate today."

"What?" Luke stared at the guard in shock, still holding the pen in his hand. "What do you mean? Who else was here?"

"I dunno, some guy. I think his name is there in the log. He just left an hour and a half ago."

A chill snaked down her spine as she stepped up to see the logbook.

The name scrawled beside Paul Sherman's was none other than Willie Johannes, the seventy-two-year-old man who died two years ago.

The same stolen identification used by the man who'd run her off the road.

TWELVE

"Describe him for me," Luke demanded in a no-nonsense tone. He could barely contain his excitement.

For a minute the guard frowned. "Average-looking guy, about five-nine or five-ten, with short brown hair, glasses. Wore jeans and a casual T-shirt."

"How old?"

"I don't know, anywhere from twenty-five to thirty-five. I didn't think too much about it."

"Do you have video cameras? I want to see him."

"Yeah, we probably have him on tape." Suddenly the guard seemed to realize there was more to his questions than idle curiosity. "Uh, I think I'd better get my supervisor."

"Good idea." Luke wasn't going to leave here without seeing this guy, and if that meant he'd have to call to get in touch with a judge to get a court order, he would. The mayor would certainly support him, now that they finally had a lead. Getting a picture of their suspect would be huge.

"Do you think it's possible there really is a Willie Johannes involved in this?" Megan asked, her freckles standing out dramatically against her pale skin.

"No. I think he's toying with us again. Only this time, he made a mistake." He didn't bother to hide his satisfaction. "We're on to him now, Megan."

The supervisor came out and introduced himself. "I'm Grayson Lang. I understand you're here investigating a murder?"

"Yes." Luke quickly filled the guard in on the events to date. "If you could show us your video of Sherman's visitor, I'd appreciate it. We have strong reason to believe he's our top suspect."

"All right. Come this way." Grayson Lang led them through the back door to the private, interior offices of the prison. They went down the hall to a small room where a guard sat, surrounded by video screens. "Josh, pull up the tape from about two hours ago, would you?"

Josh glanced over at them and then nodded. "Sure." His fingers worked the controls. "Watch here," he said, tapping the center console.

Luke practically held his breath as they watched the entrance of the prison. Finally they saw the man the guard behind the desk had described. Josh froze the image on the screen.

"Does he look familiar?" Luke asked glancing at Megan.

She slowly shook her head. "I never saw him before in my life."

He'd never seen the guy either, but at least they had a face to go with the fake name, which was more than they had a few minutes ago. "Would you make a copy of this for me?" he asked Grayson.

The supervisor hesitated for a moment, and then

shrugged. "Can you get me a court order? Or at least a formal request?"

"If I have to." He was already pulling out his phone. "I'd also like a copy of the audiotape of their conversation," Luke added, as he waited for Judge Hennepin to answer. The more he thought about it, the more he realized it would be far better to go through the legal routes to make sure there were no loopholes in the case later.

Luke got the court order from Judge Hennepin, who promised to fax it immediately. The moment the fax came through, the DVD with the video recording of the guy walking into the prison, along with a copy of the Willie Johannes signature on the logbook, were handed over.

"Do you still want to see the prisoner?" Grayson asked.

"Yes." Luke didn't hesitate for a moment. He was anxious to hear the audiotape of the conversation between their suspect and Sherman, but there would be plenty of time for that later.

Grayson nodded and led them back through the offices to the visitation area. "Okay, have a seat in cubicle number two and we'll bring the prisoner up to the holding area," he instructed.

"Thanks for all your help," Luke said, holding out his hand.

Grayson looked surprised and then returned the handshake. "You're welcome. I only hope it helps."

Luke silently agreed as he moved across the room to the visiting area, taking a seat at the table labeled number two, separated by the prisoner's side with bulletproof glass.

Their suspect had made one mistake, but he was still

puzzled by the timing. How was it that this guy managed to stay one step ahead of them? No one outside
the sheriff's department, not even his son, Sam, had
known he and Megan had decided to drive to the prison
today.

And somehow, he couldn't make himself believe the
visits fell so close together by mere coincidence.

Icy fear slithered from the back of his neck down the
center of his spine. Was it possible someone inside the
sheriff's department was involved in this? Maybe one
of the deputies who wanted his position?

No, almost as soon as the suspicion formed, he discarded it. The theory didn't make sense. Any of the deputies who wanted the job could simply run against him
in the election polls in the fall. The townspeople would
certainly support one of their own against an outsider
like Luke.

The only other possibility was that both he and
Megan were being watched. That theory was only
slightly less worrisome.

"I'm nervous," Megan whispered, as they waited for
Sherman to be brought to the visitor area.

"Don't be." He turned his attention toward Megan,
giving her fingers a reassuring squeeze. "We're perfectly
safe surrounded by all the guards."

She frowned and shook her head. "It's not that…"
Her voice trailed off when the door opened and a tall,
skinny man dressed in orange, his wrists and ankles
cuffed, shuffled into the room. He took the seat across
from them, his gaze cold.

Defiant.

Luke glanced at Megan, noting how she watched
Sherman warily. Obviously it wasn't easy for her to

face her sister's murderer, even knowing justice had been served. He looked at Sherman, forcing a congenial smile. "My name is Sheriff Luke Torretti, and I have a few questions I'd like to ask," he said, opening up the interview.

Sherman's mouth twisted into a smirk. "Ask whatever you want, I got nuthin' to say to either of you."

"That's too bad, since we came all this way to see you," Luke said lightly, refusing to show any distress. "Sounds like you've been busy, though. You've already had one visitor today, haven't you?" Luke asked. "Willie Johannes?"

Sherman cocked a brow, but didn't answer. The way he sat there, glaring at them, didn't give Luke much hope that they'd get anything out of him.

But he wasn't going to give up that easily. Life in prison had to be lonely. Even a cop visiting would be a distraction from the boredom. "Have you heard about the murder of Liza Campbell in Crystal Lake, Wisconsin?" Luke asked idly. "Whoever killed her is using your modus operandi."

Sherman opened his mouth as if to respond, but then caught himself and pressed his lips firmly together. It was clear he was fighting to remain silent.

Luke stared at the man, trying to think of a way to get through to him. In his experience most criminals liked to talk about themselves. How smart they were. How well they were able to elude the authorities.

Although the fact that Sherman was sitting in prison only proved the guy wasn't very smart.

"Come on, Sherman. Are you really going to sit there and tell me it doesn't bug you that some other guy is copying your crimes?" Luke asked. "Or maybe you and

Willie have cooked up this scheme together, huh? Is that It?"

Again, Sherman looked as if he might answer, catching himself at the last second.

They were so close. Luke could feel it. He racked his brain for some way to break through Sherman's wall of self-imposed silence.

"Paul, why won't you talk to us?" Megan asked, leaning forward, her gaze intent.

"Because you don't listen, no matter what I say," Sherman answered abruptly. "I tried to tell you I didn't kill those other girls—but you wouldn't listen."

Luke tried to hide his surprise. "Does that mean you admit to killing Megan's sister, Katie?"

Sherman shrugged and looked away. "Guard?" he called out "This visit is over. I wanna return to my cell."

"Wait, don't go back yet," Megan said urgently. "I'm sorry if I didn't listen before, but I promise to listen now."

The door opened with a loud buzz as the lock released. A burly overweight guard walked through the doorway.

"Please," Megan implored Sherman.

"Too late," Sherman hissed as he rose to his feet. "You should have listened to me before the trial. Now it's just too late."

Luke tried to assimilate what Sherman meant by that crack, not that it mattered much, as Sherman made it clear the brief visit was over. He shuffled out of the visiting area without so much as a backward glance at either of them.

Megan sat looking stunned as she stared after him.

Luke put his hand under her elbow, urging her to stand. "Come on, Megan, let's go."

She followed him back to the main desk with obvious reluctance. As Luke signed the logbook, indicating the time he left, he looked again at the bold signature of Willie Johannes.

Seems like Willie didn't stay long either, barely six minutes. And some of that time was likely spent waiting for Sherman to be brought out.

"We need to listen to the audio of the conversation between them," Luke murmured as he escorted Megan back outside.

"I know. Too bad we didn't bring a computer with us."

"We'll find the nearest library," Luke decided, unable to wait for the couple of hours it would take to get all the way back to Crystal Lake. He plugged in the data on his squad car's GPS system and discovered the nearest library was ten miles away.

Luke followed the directions, glancing over at Megan, who seemed withdrawn after seeing Sherman. He reached for her hand. "Hey, are you all right?"

"Sure." Her pathetic attempt at a smile only concerned him more. "Do you think what he said is possible?"

"What?" Luke frowned. "You mean that he didn't kill those other girls?"

"Yes." The expression on her face was one of pure agony. "What if I convicted the wrong man?"

Luke didn't want to admit that Sherman's brief confession had gotten under his skin, too. "Megan, don't torture yourself. The man murdered your sister. His DNA was found imbedded beneath her fingernails. The jury found him guilty."

"I know. But he sounded almost believable."

"Don't fall for his act," Luke advised. He pulled up in front of the library. "I'm sure once we listen to this audiotape, we'll know just how innocent Paul Sherman isn't."

They walked into the library and crossed over to the media center. He pulled up two chairs in front of one computer and picked up two sets of headphones. In minutes he had the CD plugged in and running.

"Who are you?" Luke recognized Sherman's insolent tone.

"Willie Johannes," a second voice answered.

"I don't know anyone named Willie Johannes. Why are you here? What do you want?"

"Some guy paid me a hundred bucks to come visit you. He told me I had to come and sign in as Willie Johannes. If you don't want to talk, I'll leave. No skin off my back."

"Why did someone pay you to visit me?"

"I don't know, and I don't care. A hundred bucks is a hundred bucks. Easiest money I ever made."

"Get lost. I'm not interested in whatever game you're playing. Guard? Guard! This visit's over!"

The audiotape ended as abruptly as it had begun. Luke swallowed a surge of frustration as he ripped off his headphones. "It's a setup. This guy isn't the murderer. He was paid to visit Sherman in prison. The entire visit was a setup."

Megan gazed up at him, her eyes wide and puzzled. "I heard. But why?"

"I don't know," Luke answered grimly. "But apparently you and I aren't the only pawns in the game. And that's exactly what this murder investigation is starting to feel like. Nothing but a ridiculous, deadly game."

Megan had agreed to stop for lunch on the way home, but after Luke pulled into a family-style restaurant and they took their seats, she stared at the menu, unable to find anything remotely appealing.

Listening to the audiotape had ruined her appetite. Or maybe it was their brief interaction with Paul Sherman. Either way, she finally settled on soup and a half sandwich, hoping that she'd be able to eat once the food arrived.

Bad enough that she'd had to face her sister's killer again, but the way his words kept echoing in her mind had begun to haunt her.

I didn't kill those other two girls.

During the trial, she'd listened to Sherman claim he was innocent. She didn't remember him ever claiming that he hadn't killed the first two victims. They'd found his DNA beneath Katie's fingernails. And they'd found Rohypnol in his apartment, along with a glass bottle of ether, his fingerprints all over it.

The ether in his apartment had clinched his involvement in the first two murders. A jury of twelve people had convicted Paul Sherman of all three murders.

Why would he suddenly claim he was innocent of the first two?

"Hey, are you okay?" Luke asked, breaking into her troubled thoughts.

"I don't know," she honestly admitted. "I just don't know what to think."

"We'll get to the bottom of this, Megan. We'll find the guy who took a hundred dollars to visit Sherman in jail and hopefully he can give us some sort of description. Don't worry, we'll find him."

Looking up into Luke's serious dark gaze, she believed him. Luke was a very good cop. Her investigative skills were rusty. She hadn't even thought about asking for a tape.

When their meal arrived, she was a little surprised when Luke took a moment to bow his head and pray. As a child she remembered her parents praying before every meal, so she silently murmured the same words her parents had taught her. When she finished, Luke was smiling at her.

She flushed and tried to ignore the effect his mere smile had on her senses. This wasn't the time to think about her personal feelings. Not when they had a killer playing games with them, taunting them.

She did her best to eat, even though the soup tasted like wallpaper paste and the sandwich like sawdust. She could feel Luke's gaze on her, so she tried to eat enough that he wouldn't comment.

Once they finished, Luke paid the bill so they could head back home.

Home. She surprised herself with the thought. Up until now, she hadn't really thought of Crystal Lake as home.

She'd come to the small town to heal. To find herself again. To get away from the media circus surrounding the trial.

Was she really considering staying?

Dear Lord, help guide me on the right path. Amen.

The silent prayer was almost as surprising as thinking

of Crystal Lake as home. Luke and his faith were rubbing off on her.

Or maybe, God was reminding her that He hadn't given up on her. That He'd always be there, no matter what. All she needed to do was pray.

The knowledge brought an overwhelming sense of peace.

"So what are our next steps?" she asked Luke, turning the conversation back to the investigation. "Do we go back to our theory that someone close to Paul is acting out of revenge?"

"Maybe," Luke slowly agreed. "Although truthfully, that theory doesn't feel right."

"I know." She let out a heavy sigh. "I can't seem to grasp what the killer is searching for. Most serial killers want power or control over their victims. They keep killing because they can't survive without that feeling of power and control. This crime, with the way he's taunting us as investigators, doesn't fit the mold at all."

"No, it doesn't. Which means we have to change the mold."

Startled, she glanced at him. "What do you mean?"

"He's taunting us, right?" When she nodded, he continued. "So that means the crimes aren't so much about killing as they are getting away with the crime."

For a split second, the theory made sense. Or at least, she thought it did. "So in other words, he's trying to show us how smart he is."

"He's trying to prove how much smarter he is compared to us," Luke corrected. "He's feeling superior, watching us, laughing at us, as he leads us on a wild-goose chase."

She couldn't suppress a shiver. Nor could she deny

that Luke's theory made sense. "Okay, but how does that help us find him?" she asked, fighting a wave of help-lessness.

"That's the million-dollar question, isn't it?"

"I'd rather have a clue than a million dollars," she muttered.

Luke chuckled. "Yeah, me too."

She sat back against the seat, watching the scenery whiz by. As they came closer to Crystal Lake, she sat up straighter. "Uh, Luke? Would you mind swinging by my cabin on the way home?"

"Sure thing," he agreed readily enough. "Did you forget something?"

She blushed a bit and shrugged. "I know Sunday is several days away yet, but I thought it would be a good idea to have something nice to wear to church. I felt a bit out of place last weekend."

"You looked fine," he said. The way his gaze lingered warmly on her face made her wonder if Luke was imag-ining what she'd look like in a dress. Up until now, she'd worn nothing but T-shirts and jeans.

She secretly admitted she wanted to look nice for Luke as much as she wanted to dress appropriately for church. A dress and sandals weren't too much to ask, were they? "Still, if it's not too much trouble, I'd like to pick up a few things."

"It's no trouble," he assured her. "Your cabin is on the way into town."

The rest of the drive went by in a comfortable silence. She began to yawn, her eyelids drooping with fatigue. As Luke neared her cabin, she forced the exhaustion away.

She climbed out of the car, taking a moment to

stretch her legs gratefully. Luke's cell phone rang and she waited while he answered it.

His expression turned serious and she tensed, hoping he wasn't getting bad news. "Thanks, Frank."

"What is it?" she asked with trepidation.

"They found the dark green car that ran you off the road, it was abandoned in a subdivision of Madison. Apparently they're dusting it for prints now, but so far haven't found anything."

Another dead end. She nodded, knowing there wasn't much more they could do.

Luke headed up to her front door and she quickened her pace to catch up.

"Do you have your key?" he asked, turning to face her as she joined him on the porch.

"Yes." She rolled her eyes when he held out his hand. Rather than argue about how she was perfectly able to unlock the door herself, she handed over the key.

After unlocking and opening the door, he held her back so he could go inside first. Even though she was right behind him, the rancid stench nearly knocked her off her feet.

She gasped and halted dead in her tracks, even as Luke clamped a hand on her arm to stop her.

Because she knew, only too well, the source of the horrid smell. Something she'd never gotten used to in all her years of crime scene investigating.

The unmistakable stench of a dead, decaying body.

THIRTEEN

Megan didn't protest when Luke hustled her back out to the squad car. It was all she could do to stop herself from being violently sick. She listened as he used the radio to call for a team of deputies to secure the scene.

"Wait here," he told her, moving to get out of the car.

She pushed the nausea away and reached out to grab his arm. "No! Don't go in there alone. Wait for backup."

Luke hesitated and then shook his head. "I can't believe he's hanging around inside, not with that smell. Besides, waiting inside to jump at me isn't his style. He's playing a game, remember?"

She did remember. She didn't understand, couldn't comprehend why the killer was intent on playing games.

"Stay here," he repeated. "I'll be fine."

She didn't have the energy to argue. Instead, she warily watched him go back inside the house, shivering in spite of the warm temperature. Even inside the squad car, with the doors locked and the windows rolled up, she felt exposed. Vulnerable.

When the first deputy arrived, she relaxed a little. At

least now Luke wasn't alone. She couldn't get the horrible smell out of her head, so she opened the passenger-side window, desperate for fresh air.

Within minutes, the area around her small cabin was swarming with cops. She'd lost count, but it seemed as if every deputy had responded to Luke's call. One of them stopped at the car and handed her a camera through the open window. She watched as they carefully and deliberately fanned out, making sure they covered the entire area, talking to each other on the radios clipped to their collars.

In her lap she held the camera, her fingers slick with sweat as she gripped it tightly in her hand.

Soon it would be her turn. Once the deputies secured the premises she would take the crime scene photos. She wasn't at all certain she could do it.

When Luke came back outside she forced herself to get out of the car to meet him halfway, searching his grim expression.

"Another young girl?" she asked, dreading the answer.

He nodded. "Young and blonde, just like Liza. I've seen her around, her name is Amy Schiller. She waitresses on the weekends at Rose's Café." He sighed and scrubbed a hand over his jaw. "I need to get in touch with her parents."

She remembered the young blonde who'd served her the veggie lasagna the night she'd met Jake. Was that the same girl? Her stomach clenched. She'd been so pretty. So young. Her whole life ahead of her.

She didn't envy Luke's conversation with her parents. She forced herself to think and act like a crime scene investigator. "How long has she been dead?"

Luke shook his head. "I'm not sure. I'm no expert, but from the smell I would have guessed a long time. Maybe even twenty-four hours. Yet it doesn't seem like she's been inside your house for that length of time. Maybe a couple of hours."

Her heart stuttered in her chest. Her house. The killer had put the body of his latest victim, poor Amy Schiller, in her house.

Her knees threatened to give away, but she locked them in place with effort. The deputies had searched the immediate area without finding any trace of the killer. Yet he'd been inside her house, not just once when he'd left the message on her mirror, but again today.

And after everything that had happened, she couldn't discount the probability that he was hiding somewhere, watching them with binoculars.

Isn't that what a killer who enjoyed playing mind games would do?

The tiny hairs on the back of her neck rose, and she resisted the urge to glance over her shoulder. "Okay." It took every iota of willpower she possessed to step around Luke to head inside her small cabin.

"Megan." Luke's low, husky voice stopped her. She turned to face him, her gaze questioning. "You don't have to do this."

"Yes, I do." This message left by the killer was even more blatant and bold than assaulting the first victim in her backyard. He wanted her to go inside, to find the body of young Amy, which he'd left in her house.

The killer wanted her to suffer as much as his victims.

Feeling like a mere puppet whose master was yanking on her strings, she slowly approached her front door and stepped inside.

The deputy posted just inside the doorway nodded at her as she walked in. She tore her eyes from his resigned gaze and forced herself to walk down the hall, knowing instinctively the body would be in her bedroom.

In her bed.

She tripped, stumbling against the wall. In some remote portion of her mind, she realized she'd never be able to live in this cabin again.

When she reached the doorway of her bedroom, she paused and swept an intent gaze over the area. She took her time, unwilling to miss any potential clue. She raised her camera, and looking through the viewfinder helped steady her. Work. Focus on work. She took several photos to document the scene.

She recognized the young waitress. As Luke had mentioned, Amy was slender and blonde. She looked young, far too young to have lost her life to violence. As she'd suspected, the body was positioned purposefully on her bed. The orange polyurethane hollow-braided rope he'd used to kill her was still lying across her neck.

She braced herself for a flashback, but this time her mind didn't fail her. She remained firmly in the present. This wasn't about Katie anymore.

It was about Amy. And Liza. The most recent victims, whose families deserved closure.

She dragged her gaze from the young girl to look at the rest of her room. All of her things seemed just as she'd left them. In fact, Amy's body was lying on top of the thin blanket on her neatly made bed.

He hadn't killed her here in her house. In some distant

portion of her mind, she realized they'd need to search for the area where she'd died. Another struggle in the backyard? Or someplace else?

She stood there, knowing she needed to go farther inside the room to do her job. To see if Amy had DNA evidence of her killer anywhere on her body.

Lord, give me strength.

Luke came up behind her, startling her with his presence as he gently rested his broad hands on her shoulders. "I'm right here," he murmured.

She was extremely grateful for his support, and it occurred to her that God had sent Luke to provide the strength she needed.

With renewed determination, she entered the room and began the painstaking, detailed job of collecting evidence. All the while she was hoping and praying she'd find something to use against the killer in court once Luke and his deputies had him in custody.

Megan and the deputy who'd dusted for prints finished with the crime scene a good two hours later. But the job had been far from satisfying.

She couldn't help the sinking feeling that her efforts had been in vain.

There had been a glaring lack of clues. Nothing at all like the few things they'd found on Liza. Oh, there had been a couple of hairs on the floor of her bedroom and in her bathroom, but they were the same auburn color as hers, so she wasn't getting her hopes up that the killer had made a mistake, leaving something incriminating behind. Amy's fingernails appeared to be clear as well, even though they'd go through the formal testing process to make sure. And she would instruct the team to search for traces of Rohypnol and ether.

There hadn't been a thread or a fiber out of place. The crime scene was clean.

Exceptionally clean.

"I don't understand," Luke murmured, frustration lining his face. "If I didn't know any better, I'd swear this perp has some sort of police background. Otherwise we'd find something, wouldn't we?"

The idea that the killer might be someone with a law-enforcement or criminal-investigation background made her feel sick to her stomach. But he was right. "This is very odd. Usually there is something left behind," she admitted slowly.

The rest of her house looked untouched, even though they'd dusted every surface. The killer had jimmied the back door, carried Amy inside and then left again.

There was no denying she was still bothered by what Sherman had told them. Troubled, she turned to face Luke. "You know, there wasn't anything left behind at the first two crime scenes either."

Luke narrowed his gaze. "You mean the crime scenes of Sherman's first two victims?"

She nodded. The similarities between Amy's murder and the first two girls were downright eerie. They would have to wait for the autopsy, of course, but somehow she suspected that Amy had been given ether instead of Rohypnol, just like the first two victims.

Something vague tugged at her memory. She frowned and tried to concentrate on the previous crime scenes, knowing she was missing something important.

"Sheriff?" They were interrupted by one of the deputies, who approached Luke's squad car where they both stood. "Amy Schiller's parents have called the dispatcher to report her missing. They're pretty hysterical."

Of course they were. They had good reason to be hysterical.

"I'm on my way," Luke assured the deputy.

She glanced at Luke with sympathy. "Do you want me to come with you?"

He hesitated and then shook his head. "No, it's probably best if I go alone. What I really need is for you to go back to headquarters to keep working on this case. These crimes have to be related to Sherman's victims. Maybe your initial theory was right and the copycat killer is re-creating the crimes of Sherman's earlier victims. They're related, but I need your help to figure out how they're connected."

"All right, I'll do my best." She watched Luke walk away, her heart going out to him and to Amy Schiller's family.

As she slid into the passenger seat of the deputy's vehicle, she could only hope Luke's faith in her abilities wasn't misplaced.

Luke pulled up into the Schillers' driveway, his stomach knotted with dread.

This part of the job never got any easier.

Amy's parents had obviously been watching for him, because they met him outside when he climbed from the squad car.

"What do *you* want?" Greg Schiller asked in a tone that was clearly hostile.

Luke didn't let their anger faze him. After all, they had every right to be upset.

He'd failed to protect their daughter. Failed to find Liza's murderer in time to save Amy.

And nothing he was going to say today would change that fact.

He gazed at them solemnly. "Mr. and Mrs. Schiller, it might be best if we talk inside."

"We're fine right here," Greg Schiller said harshly. "You're not welcome in our home. In fact, I'd prefer to have someone else take our statement."

Luke was a little surprised by Greg's vehemence against him personally. After all, they were all members of the same church congregation. But he truly understood their anger. They clearly thought they were giving a statement about their missing daughter. They likely assumed he was slacking off in his job as interim sheriff.

The worst part of all was that they had no idea the bad news he'd come to deliver.

He shifted his weight from one foot to the other, wishing there was a kinder, gentler way to tell them. "I'm afraid I have bad news. We found Amy, she—"

"No," Robin Schiller interrupted. "No, don't say it." Her face went pale and she clutched her husband's arm tightly. "Amy is alive. She's fine. She was staying overnight at a friend's house and must have decided to walk home. She'll be here any minute. Do you hear me?" her voice rose to a hysterical level. "She's fine!"

He couldn't imagine the pain of losing a child. "I'm sorry," he said helplessly. "Let's go inside…"

"No! What are you saying?" Greg asked harshly. "She's dead? Our baby, our Amy, is dead?"

"I'm sorry," Luke said again. "We found her just a couple of hours ago. She was strangled, just like Liza

Campbell. We'll need you to come down to formally identify her."

Robin Schiller's keening wail filled the air as she collapsed against her husband, sobbing uncontrollably. Helplessly, Luke wished he could give them something to ease their pain.

But they didn't have a clue. Not one bit of evidence to give them any idea how and where to find this homicidal maniac.

How long before he killed again?

"Is there anything I can do for you? Someone you'd like me to call?" Luke finally asked.

"Haven't you already done enough?" Greg demanded, glaring at him over his wife's shoulder with grief-stricken eyes. "It's obvious your son is responsible for this. Get off my property, *Sheriff*. Better yet, go back to Milwaukee and take that no-good son with you!"

Luke could only stand there and gape at them in shock as Greg Schiller dragged his wife back inside the house and slammed the door.

Reeling from Greg Schiller's verbal assault, Luke drove back to the sheriff's department headquarters.

He replayed the scene over and over in his mind, feeling as if he'd missed something. He'd seen many reactions to grief, but this personal attack was by far the worst. Very unexpected from a couple he often saw seated in the front row of church.

Was it possible other Crystal Lake residents felt the same way as the Schillers? But if so, why? Why on earth would they consider Sam a murder suspect? Granted, he'd been disturbed at how his son was the last one to see Liza alive and that he didn't have an alibi for the time frame of Liza's murder, but that didn't mean Sam had killed the girl.

So why point the finger at his son?

Even as the thoughts whirled through his mind, he knew the answer. Because Sam was an outsider. Because his son looked and dressed differently from the other kids. Because Sam didn't have a lot of friends.

His son was easy prey.

Abruptly, he slammed his foot on the brakes and spun around in an illegal U-turn to head back home.

He needed to talk to Sam. Now. Before news of his assumed guilt spread through the town like wildfire.

His heart was hammering in his chest when he pulled up into the driveway. Sam's truck was still gone, and he could only assume Doug still had it.

He hoped and prayed Sam was at home. He wanted to talk to Sam before anyone else did. Thank God his son had been home last night.

But not the night before, a tiny voice in the back of his mind reminded him.

Not the night before.

Don't think about it, he told himself sternly. They didn't know the time frame of when Amy was killed. No need to automatically think the worst. The Schillers would have sounded the alarm much sooner if Amy had been missing for two days.

He parked the squad car in the driveway and practically ran inside the house.

"Sam? Are you home?" he called as he headed for his son's room.

Empty. Sam wasn't in his room or out on the deck or in the kitchen.

Reining in a flash of panic, he mentally smacked

himself in the head. Of course Sam wasn't home. Why hadn't he remembered Sam was working the early shift at the diner?

Muttering under his breath, he went back outside and drove into town. Main Street was packed with tourists, so he parked down by Barry's Pub and then walked the few blocks to Rose's Café.

The place was filled with people, mostly tourists from the way they ignored him, but it didn't take long for him to catch Josie's attention behind the counter. "Can I talk to Sam?" he shouted over the din.

"Sorry, sweetie, but you already missed him," Josie said, her gaze apologetic. "He left about fifteen or twenty minutes ago."

"Thanks." Fifteen or twenty minutes. Certainly plenty of time to get home, if that happened to be his son's destination.

But since he'd just come from home, it obviously wasn't.

Outside, he jogged down to the squad car. Okay, Sam wasn't at home or at work. Which left Doug's house. If his son wasn't hanging out with his friend, then he'd really have reason to panic.

Thankfully the ride to Doug's house wasn't far. And when he saw Sam's rusted black truck parked in the driveway, he felt an overwhelming sense of relief.

Sam was probably here. No doubt Doug had picked him up from work. He parked and then slowly peeled his clenched fingers from the steering wheel.

For a moment he sat in the squad car, trying to pull himself together and wiping the remnants of worry off his face. When he opened the car door and stepped out onto the blacktop driveway, the front door of Doug's house slammed open and Sam came barreling out.

"Is it true?" his son demanded, his eyes wild and hands clenched into fists.

Luke winced at the raw agony in Sam's voice. Obviously the news of Amy's death and that Sam might be a suspect had already spread through the town faster than a highly contagious virus.

"Yes." Luke reached out to put a calming hand on his son's shoulder, but Sam violently shook him off as if he couldn't stand to be touched. Helplessly he watched Sam's body tremble with anger. "I'm sorry, son. I'm so sorry."

"No!" Sam spun on his heel and slammed his fist onto the hood of the squad car with such force he left an unmistakable dent. *"Not Amy!"*

Luke frowned and took a step toward his son. Sam continued to pace in Doug's front yard, his eyes welling up with tears.

"Not Amy, not Amy," Sam repeated over and over, grasping his hair as if he were going to rip it out by the roots.

The tears and the writhing agony weren't fake. Alarm bells clamored in his head. Something was wrong. Desperately wrong. Sam hadn't reacted this way when he'd heard the news about Liza Campbell.

Apparently Amy was more to Sam than *some stupid chick.*

And suddenly the animosity of Amy's parents made sense. It wasn't that he was there to deliver the bad news, but because he was Sam's father. Amy's parents didn't like Luke because he was the town troublemaker's father.

"You have to find this guy, Dad," Sam shouted, whirling around to face him. "Do you hear me? Amy was innocent! She didn't deserve this. She was the best thing that ever happened to me!"

The nagging suspicion couldn't be denied. "Sam, what are you saying? Was Amy your girlfriend?" he asked hoarsely.

FOURTEEN

"Yeah. She and I—*Amy*." Sam broke down again, this time full-out sobbing. His sorrow ripped at Luke. The last time he'd seen his son react like this had been at his mother's funeral.

Helplessly, he tried to think of something to say. He was stunned beyond belief to discover his son had a girlfriend. Why hadn't he said anything? Brought her over to meet him? Had they been seeing each other secretly?

Because Amy's parents had disapproved of the relationship?

As much as the idea made him mad, he was forced to acknowledge the possibility that Amy's parents weren't thrilled with Sam. Even Megan had considered him trouble when she'd first seen him. His son hadn't tried to fit in here at Crystal Lake.

Yet none of that mattered anymore, now that Amy was dead.

Murdered.

The chilling reality of the situation sank in. Amy's parents suspected Sam of killing their daughter.

And once the news of their secret romance leaked out, everyone else in town would suspect his son too.

Panic compelled him forward. "Sam, listen to me. If you want to help Amy, you need to talk to me."

Sam whirled on his father. "Help her? She's *dead!* I should have protected her!"

"No, you listen to me." Luke tightly grasped his son's shoulders, forcing Sam to meet his gaze. "I need your help to find the man who did this. Do you understand? I need your help, Sam. You knew Amy better than anyone else."

His words finally seemed to reach through the depths of Sam's grief. Sam swiped his face against the sleeve of his T-shirt and pulled himself together. He pinned Luke with a fierce gaze. "All right. I'll help you. What do you want to know?"

"Not here," Luke cautioned, glancing over to the doorway of Doug's house where Lynette and Doug stood, watching Sam with sympathetic faces. How long before they believed the worst of Sam too? Luke shuddered at the thought. "We need to talk somewhere private."

Sam tensed for a moment, as if he were about to argue, but then his shoulders slumped and he gave an abrupt nod. "Can we go home, Dad?"

The simple request held an unmistakable longing that nearly cut Luke off at the knees. For the first time in longer than he could remember, he felt like a father.

He threw his arm around Sam's shoulders to give him a brief embrace. "Of course we can go home."

In the squad car, Luke shot several worried glances over at Sam as he drove. Sam still looked badly shaken, but there was a determined glint in his son's eyes that hadn't been there before.

Luke understood why. The case had turned personal

now. For both of them. Sam wanted to avenge his girl-friend's death and Luke was determined to prove his son's innocence, no matter what.

When Luke pulled into his driveway, he was sur-prised to find Megan there, waiting on the front porch. He couldn't hide the rush of relief when he saw her.

"What is she doing here?" Sam asked, his brows pulled together in a frown.

"I wasn't expecting her, but she's probably here on official business. She's part of this investigation, remem-ber?" Luke said, glancing at his son. "And she's a CSI expert." He forced himself to put his son's needs before his own. Maybe Sam didn't want to pour his soul out in front of a woman. "If you want me to send her away, I will."

There was a slight pause, but then Sam slowly shook his head. "No, you're right, she is the expert. She can stay. For now."

Luke climbed from the squad car and Megan rose to her feet to meet them halfway. "Hi. Uh, Amy's par-ents called the station." She sent a quick glance at Sam, a hint of empathy darkening her gaze. "I came over to lend my support."

The unspoken words in her worried face made him realize she knew exactly what had transpired when he'd given Amy's parents the bad news. The knot in his gut tightened painfully. He shouldn't be surprised that Amy's parents were throwing their accusations against Sam around publicly, but he'd hoped to keep that under wraps for a while yet.

"Let's go inside," he suggested.

The sullen expression was back on Sam's face as they all trooped into the living room. Luke steeled himself against another wave of sympathy. The father in him longed to give Sam the time and the privacy to grieve.

But they were running out of time. The best thing he could do for Sam right now was find the real murderer.

"Tell me the last time you saw Amy," Luke said as he faced his son. "And Sam, it's important that you tell us everything. I can't help you if there are facts I don't know."

Sam sat on the edge of the chair, his elbows braced on his knees, his gaze trained on the carpet. "I'm sure you figured out I met Amy at Rose's Café. We secretly started seeing each other a couple of months ago."

Luke noticed Megan didn't seem surprised by his son's revelation. Her reaction gave him a clue about what Amy's parents were saying.

"Her parents were pretty strict, Amy had to be home by eleven when she wasn't working, even on weekends, so we didn't get together very often. But her best friend, Janice, covered for her a lot so we could see each other."

When Sam paused, obviously still mired in grief, Luke gently nudged him. "Were you with her last weekend?"

"Saturday night," Sam admitted. "I told you I went to the bonfire, but I was really with Amy, that's why I was walking home so late. She sneaked out of her house to meet me."

"Did you go anywhere in particular?" he pressed, wondering if anyone else had seen Amy and Sam together.

"No, I didn't want her to go anywhere alone, not with this psycho guy running loose, so we met in her backyard, down by the lake. Eventually she went back inside and I walked home. But the more I thought about it, the madder I got about the whole thing. We shouldn't have to sneak around. I was tired of hiding my feelings for her. So I went to see her on Sunday at the café, before she started her shift. We argued, because she refused to tell her parents she liked me and wanted to go out with me."

Luke could hear the underlying hint of pain in Sam's tone. He could only imagine how hard it would be to know that your girlfriend didn't want her parents to know the truth. But somehow they must have known, otherwise, why would they resent Sam so much? To the point of blaming Sam for their daughter's murder?

"Sam, they knew the truth," Luke said, trying to break the news gently. "They knew Amy was seeing you."

"Only because she told them," Sam said defensively. "Right after that detective finished interviewing me, Amy called. She was crying, because she'd called her parents while on break at the diner and told them about us. They weren't just a little mad, they went totally crazy. Told her she couldn't see me anymore. Threatened to make her quit her job at the café and to take her car away." Sam's tone, mired in sheer agony, ripped at his heart. "They hated me, more than I realized," he said in a low tone.

Luke stared at Sam, trying to think of something to say. He should have given his son the benefit of the doubt, because suddenly the pieces of the puzzle fell into place. "That was the reason you and Doug took off to go camping by the abandoned farm, wasn't it? Not because of the interview with Frank, but because you were upset over how Amy's parents took the news."

Sam scrubbed his hands over his face and nodded. "Maybe I went a little crazy myself. I wanted to leave this stupid town, leave without looking back. But eventually Doug talked me out of it. I realized that even if Amy broke up with me, I didn't want to leave without ever seeing her again."

Luke briefly closed his eyes, knowing God had responded to his prayers. He made a mental note to thank Doug, too. He tried to bring his focus back to the details of the murder investigation. "So what time exactly did you see Amy on Sunday?"

"She had to work at three-thirty in the afternoon, but she told her parents she had to work at three. We met in the alley behind the café."

Where no one would see them. He couldn't imagine how difficult it must have been for Sam to hide his true feelings. No wonder his son had been so secretive about where he was and what he was doing. "And how long was she scheduled to work?"

Sam lifted a shoulder helplessly. "Normally she gets off around eleven at night, but depending on how busy the café is, she might have to stay a little longer."

"But she was sixteen, right?" When Sam nodded, Luke glanced at Megan. "Federal law prohibits sixteen-year-old kids from working later than twelve-thirty at night, right?"

"Generally, yes, during the school year, but not during the summer," Megan murmured. "The hours are unlimited during the summer."

That news didn't help much, although he could easily find out from Josie what time Amy punched out from work. "The real question here is what time Amy got home on Sunday night," Luke decided. "She must have gone home, because her parents didn't call her in as missing until today."

"Maybe not," Sam said in a low voice.

"What do you mean?" Luke demanded.

"Amy called before my cell phone died. She said she wanted to come and see me at the barn. She was going to tell her parents she was at a sleepover at Janice's for two nights as a way to celebrate her birthday on Monday."

Luke stared at Sam in dismay. "But she didn't show up, did she?"

"No." Sam's voice was barely above a whisper. "I figured she changed her mind about us. One of the reasons Doug and I finally came home was so I could find her and talk to her."

Luke digested that piece of information. "So it's possible Amy's been missing since late Sunday night or early Monday morning? But we only just found out about it on Tuesday?"

"Janice wouldn't have said anything sooner, not if she assumed Amy was with me." Sam's eyes reflected the depth of his guilt.

"Oh, Sam, it's not your fault," Megan whispered.

Luke mentally echoed her sentiment, but it was no wonder Amy's parents had jumped to conclusions about Sam.

He could hardly blame them. If Sam had been anyone but his son, he might have felt the same way.

For several minutes, no one spoke. Finally Luke took out his cell phone and called Frank. "I need you to find out from the medical examiner what the estimated time of death is for Amy Schiller."

"The ME just called with the estimate," Frank admitted. "They're putting the time of her death as sometime on Monday, between four and eight in the morning."

Luke closed his eyes on a wave of despair. "Okay, thanks, Frank."

Frank continued, "We're going to have to interview your son again. He wasn't at the bonfire Saturday night and Amy's parents..."

"I know," he interrupted, not really wanting to hear the accusations all over again.

"It's only questioning at this point, but you need to know, if it comes down to it, if we arrest him, there is a good chance Sam will be tried as an adult."

An adult. Because Sam's eighteenth birthday was just a couple of weeks away. He and Shelia had held Sam back a year to make sure he would do well in school.

And now his son might be tried as an adult for a murder he didn't commit.

"Don't worry, I'll bring him in." He snapped his phone shut and glanced at Megan.

"I heard," she said softly.

"So I'm a suspect again?" Sam asked, his tone full of anger. He leaped to his feet and began to pace the short expanse of the living room with agitated motions. "I don't believe it! Doesn't Doug's word mean anything in this town? I was with him all night!"

"Of course Doug's word means something," Luke said with more confidence than he felt. "I'll take you down to the station, but you're not going to give a statement. Not until we hire a lawyer."

"A lawyer?" Sam stopped dead in his tracks, and his

face went pale. For several long moments his son stared at him incredulously. "Seriously? You really think I need a lawyer?"

Megan glanced over her shoulder at Sam, who sat hunched in the corner of the backseat of Luke's squad car staring blankly out the window.

A strained silence filled the car as they rode along the highway toward the center of town.

She couldn't think of a single encouraging word to say. The entire situation seemed surreal. She reached over to take Luke's hand in hers, a silent testament of her support. He squeezed her fingers reassuringly and flashed a strained smile.

If only there was something more she could do to help. She could only imagine what both Luke and Sam were going through.

The news of Sam's romantic involvement with the latest victim had been the hot topic of discussion down at the sheriff's department headquarters the moment the call from Amy's parents had come in.

Disturbed by what she was hearing, she'd gone to Frank, quietly asking if he'd take her to Luke's house. Thankfully, he'd agreed.

But she'd never imagined the full extent of what Sam had revealed. The secret liaisons Sam had with Amy wouldn't help his case. Even though he did have Doug as an alibi, there was plenty to worry about. The circumstantial evidence didn't look at all promising.

She'd been glad when Luke called Reed Gaston, a well-known criminal lawyer from Madison. Gaston had instantly agreed to meet them down at headquarters, cautioning Luke that Sam shouldn't say anything until he arrived.

It was too early to eat dinner, and besides that, no one was very hungry. Instead they waited a half hour before heading down to headquarters to meet Reed.

When Luke pulled into his designated parking spot, he met Sam's gaze in the rearview mirror. "Remember, you're not to say a single word until you've spoken to Reed."

"I won't."

Megan could barely stand to watch as Frank and Deputy Scott met Sam the moment he crossed the threshold of the building. The poor boy was still a teenager, but he looked as if he'd aged well beyond his years.

"This way," Frank said kindly, steering Sam toward the interrogation room. "Your attorney is inside, waiting for you."

Wordlessly, Sam followed the deputies without a backward glance at his father.

Luke stood for several long moments before he headed for his office. She followed him, unwilling to let him suffer alone. She barely managed to skirt inside the door before he shut it with a loud click.

"Luke, it's going to be okay," she murmured when he hung his head and rubbed the back of his neck. "They don't have enough evidence to arrest Sam."

"Maybe they don't need evidence," Luke said bleakly. "Everyone has already tried him and found him guilty because we're outsiders here."

She crossed over to lightly grasp his arm. "Don't say that," she said sternly. "Of course they need evidence.

They'll need something to prove Doug wrong. He isn't an outsider," she pointed out.

For several long seconds he stared down at her, and then suddenly he pulled her into his arms. She willingly clutched him close, wishing she could do more. "I'm so afraid I'll lose him," he murmured against her hair.

"You won't."

"I wish I could believe that." She could feel him rub his cheek against her hair.

She drew back just enough to gaze up at him. "We're going to find this guy, Luke. And when we do, Sam will be proven innocent."

"Your faith humbles me," he said softly.

"Your faith helped show me the way," she pointed out. "Do you really think God is going to abandon us now?"

"No." For a moment hope brightened his eyes. And then his gaze dropped to her mouth. She held her breath as anticipation swirled in her bloodstream.

"I'm so glad I found you, Megan," he said before he lowered his mouth to hers.

She melted against him, reveling in the softness, the passion of his kiss.

The door to his office suddenly swung open and Luke instantly raised his head. For a moment she couldn't concentrate, but then realized Sam had interrupted them again.

"Don't you think you should stop thinking with your hormones and start looking for Amy's murderer?" Sam asked harshly. "Or don't you care that I'm a murder suspect?"

Megan winced when she saw Luke's cheeks flush with guilt. He instantly dropped his arms and took a long step away from Megan, putting plenty of distance between them.

And worse, he staunchly avoided her gaze.

Sam let out a disgusted sigh. "Reed Gaston wants to talk to both of us, if you can manage to tear yourself away from *her*." The disdain in his tone was glaringly obvious. "Although maybe you'd be happier if I went to jail. That way I'd be out of your way for good."

"Of course not, Sam, don't be ridiculous. I'm sorry. You're absolutely right," Luke said, pushing the dagger deeper into her heart. "This is hardly the time for distractions. Let's go."

Without any sort of apology, Luke brushed past her as if she didn't even exist and followed Sam.

FIFTEEN

Ignoring the curious stares of the deputies and dispatchers working in the department, Megan lifted her chin defiantly and walked down the hall.

Only then, in the private sanctuary of the small office, did she allow the tears from Luke's rejection to slip silently down her cheeks.

He couldn't have made his feelings more clear. And even if he had felt something for her, if Sam didn't approve she knew full well that whatever feelings they might have shared wouldn't mean a thing.

Luke would never sacrifice his relationship with his son.

And truthfully, she couldn't ask him to.

After a few minutes of wallowing in self-pity, she pulled herself together with a monumental effort.

Maybe Sam was right.

Maybe they were allowing themselves to be distracted by emotions.

Another girl had died and they were no closer to finding the truth.

With renewed determination, she blew her nose and then opened the transcripts of the Sherman trial, doing what she should have done in the first place, rather than following her heart to rush to Luke's side.

There had to be a connection between the Sherman murders and the latest Crystal Lake victims.

All she had to do was to find it.

Keeping focused on the details of the crimes wasn't easy, not when she was constantly wondering how things were going with Sam and Luke. But soon she became embroiled in the past.

Abruptly stumbling across the detail that had niggled in the back of her mind earlier.

Latex. Latex was made of rather large protein particles—the reason so many hospitals had stopped using it was because the particles became airborne and tended to cause allergic reactions after repeated exposures.

Latex particles were found on the rope around Katie's neck. But not on the first two victims. No, the rope on the first two victims had revealed particles of plastic, the type that might have come from plastic gloves.

If the killer had used latex, they would have for sure found evidence of it.

Quickly, she leafed through the paperwork on Liza's autopsy. The ME had found plastic particles embedded in the rope around Liza's neck. Not latex.

Katie's murder was the outlier.

She went back to Sherman's trial transcript. Latex gloves had been found in his apartment. Not plastic gloves. She sat back, forcing the memories she'd long suppressed to surface.

At the time, they hadn't thought too much about the difference between the types of gloves. After all, it was possible Paul had used plastic with the first two victims, but then for some reason ended up wearing latex gloves with Katie. There was certainly nothing to prove otherwise.

Except Paul's claim that he hadn't committed the first two crimes.

Goose bumps rose along her arms. What if Sherman was right? What if in their haste to convict him, they hadn't done a thorough job of investigating the truth?

He'd gone to the same university as Katie. He worked in the chemistry lab, she'd worked in the library. Obviously they easily could have met at either place. Witnesses had seen him talking to Katie inside the pub. He'd spiked her drink with Rohypnol.

Was it possible the chemistry lab used latex gloves?

What if he'd killed Katie because of some personal issue between them? What if he really hadn't murdered the first two victims, but used the same M.O. to kill Katie? What if he was actually the original copycat murderer?

And the same man who'd killed the first two victims was still on the loose, killing again—while taunting her to find him?

Megan glanced at her watch. It was already close to five o'clock. The Madison crime lab would be pretty much closed down for the night, but she had a key.

They'd given her a key the last time they'd asked her to do a weekend shift. She'd forgotten to turn it back in.

Besides, the lab wasn't ever closed down completely. There was a skeleton crew on the off shifts.

Did she dare drive up to the lab to see what sorts of particles might be embedded in the braided threads of the rope used on Amy?

If she could prove that these two most recent murders

were likely linked to victims they'd found well over two years ago, she could get Sam off the suspect list. Not to mention they'd have four murders indicating the work of a serial killer, warranting a call to the FBI.

And having the FBI called in would take pressure off Luke.

She didn't want to delay, because every instinct she had was screaming at her that this was the only theory that made sense.

Taking a deep breath to calm her jangled nerves, she walked slowly out to the main area of the sheriff's department to find Luke.

He was standing off to the side, talking to Sam. She wasn't trying to eavesdrop but could tell they were discussing the interview that had already taken place.

She hung back for a few minutes, waiting for them to finish.

Luke saw her standing there and broke off his conversation with his son. "Is there something you need?" he asked politely, without any of the warmth she'd come to appreciate.

"I have a theory about our murder suspect, when you have a minute," she said.

"I'm pretty busy. Can it wait?" Luke asked.

She narrowed her gaze. Hadn't he been the one who decided they couldn't be distracted from the investigation? "Not really," she began, only to be interrupted by Frank.

"Sheriff, Mayor wants to talk to you," Frank yelled from halfway across the room.

Luke's brows came together in a deep frown. "Tell him I'll call him back."

Frank was already shaking his head. "No, sir, this

wasn't a request, but an order. He wants to see you in his office down at city hall, ASAP."

Megan saw the resigned expression in Luke's eyes as he glanced at his son, and she realized that the mayor had probably already heard about Sam's potential involvement. Obviously it wouldn't look good for the interim sheriff to have a son suspected of murder.

"Go ahead, Dad, I'll wait here for you," Sam said.

"All right. I'll be back as soon as I can," Luke said with a sigh. "I have a feeling this meeting won't take long."

Megan couldn't believe it when Luke brushed past her yet again without so much as a glance in her direction. She could feel Sam's intense gaze, gauging her reaction.

She tried to ignore them both. Okay, so Luke wasn't interested in her theory. So what? She didn't need his approval, and besides, there was no point in sitting around doing nothing.

The sooner she got her evidence, the better.

Megan hurried back down the hall to her office so she could get her purse and her car keys. Thankfully, she'd gotten a call earlier that her car was repaired. She'd noticed it sitting in the parking lot when they'd arrived.

For a moment, she hesitated, remembering how she'd been followed, but then she steeled her resolve.

No one knew her plans. The chances of anyone realizing she was heading to Madison at this late hour were slim to none.

Feeling more self-confident, she slung her purse over her shoulder and headed back out to the main dispatch area. Sam was still standing there, his shoulder propped against the wall. Aside from Sam, who glanced at her curiously, no one else seemed to pay attention to her as she slipped outside.

The parking lot wasn't too crowded, but her car was parked all the way in the back of the lot, next to another car. She walked across the asphalt, glancing up at the overcast sky.

At least this time, it didn't look like it was going to rain.

Just as she reached her car, she felt someone step up behind her. She whirled around, her heart in her throat, but then relaxed when she recognized the person as her friend and mentor.

"Raoul! You scared me." She put a hand up to her racing heart. "What on earth are you doing here?" she asked.

He didn't smile, and a shiver rippled down her back at the coldness in his eyes. But before she could move or shout, he'd covered her nose and her mouth with a cloth that reeked of ether and pressed her back against the unyielding car.

As her limbs went weak, she stared at him in horror.

Raoul Lee was the killer!

Help me, Lord! Please save me!

"You've proven to be quite disappointing, Megan," he said almost conversationally, as he yanked open the passenger door of the car beside hers and roughly shoved her inside. He stood there for several more seconds, until red dots swam in her vision. "And I'm growing tired of this game. Too bad, really, you had such potential. I honestly considered you one of my brightest pupils."

She wanted to fight, to escape, but she couldn't move. Her muscles were totally lax, as if she were paralyzed.

But when Raoul stepped away to slam the car door shut, she caught a quick glimpse of Sam's wide eyes as he watched from the doorway of the police station. Hope flared as she thought he must have realized what was going on, but then suddenly he was gone.

Sam? Come find me, Sam! Dear Lord, help me!

Her slim hope of rescue evaporated. She couldn't do anything but sit helplessly in the corner of the passenger seat as Raoul casually slid behind the wheel of the car. In a flash he had the car started and had backed out of the parking space. No one seemed to notice as he drove toward the highway.

"I can't believe how you let me down." Raoul glanced at her with an expression of pure hatred as he drove. "I trained you better than this! How stupid can you be, Megan? I mean, really, how could you ignore the evidence like that? At first I was amused when Sherman was arrested for all three murders, but then I began to grow very annoyed with you. Sherman was an idiot, but you credited him with masterminding three murders!"

She forced her eyelids open with an effort, concentrating on his face. The drug-soaked cloth he'd pressed against her face was still lying on her chest, the sweet scent making her feel sick.

"I tried to give you another chance to redeem yourself by killing Liza in your backyard, but once again, you failed miserably. How could you be so dense? Didn't you see me following you? Didn't you figure out I bugged your cell phone?"

Horrified by what Raoul was saying, she tried not to listen.

If she could move, she'd wiggle around until the cloth fell to the floor. But no matter how hard she tried, she couldn't make her muscles obey her commands. In some dark corner of her mind, she realized there must be something else mixed with the other, some sort of concoction that Raoul Lee had dreamed up himself, to hold his victims awake yet captive.

Another detail she'd missed during the investigation. First the latex particles and now this. Would her mistakes cost her her life?

Dear God, give me strength.

"Those two girls weren't my first victims, you know," he continued, as if they were actually having a rational conversation. "Do you remember me telling you how I worked in Boulder, Colorado, before coming to Chicago? I killed several young girls there, too. But I was smart enough to move on before anyone caught me. I was planning to leave Chicago, too, except that idiot Sherman decided to kill your sister, copying my M.O. I was going to kill him myself, but you had him arrested, without the opportunity of parole, before I could get to him."

As Raoul talked, telling her horrible details about the lives he'd taken, she desperately tried to think of a way to escape. God helped those who tried to help themselves, didn't He? And Raoul had obviously chosen her as his next victim, or he wouldn't be telling her all this.

He was going to kill her, the same way he'd killed all those other girls.

Dragging her gaze away from the man who'd been her teacher and her mentor, she looked out the windshield and saw a large dilapidated red barn. She vaguely remembered Sam saying something about how he and

Doug had camped near an old abandoned red barn the night he'd gotten into the fight with Amy.

When Raoul drove off the road, onto some sort of dirt trail, her hopes of being rescued diminished even further. The small clearing was surrounded by dense trees. No way would anyone think to look for her here.

If they even decided to look for her at all.

"I have already accepted a job offer in Seattle," he told her as he turned off the car. "So once I'm finished with you, I'll leave town and no one will ever link your death, and the deaths of those two ridiculous girls, to me."

The gleam of insanity in his eyes sent a chill down her back. Because he was right. His plan seemed almost foolproof. Not only would Raoul escape but poor Sam might be wrongly convicted of the crimes.

Raoul's crimes.

"This is all your fault, you know," he continued, after he'd pulled a blanket out of the trunk and come over to open her passenger door. "You never should have dumped me for Jake Feeney. Pathetic how he came up here, begging you to take him back. At least you were smart enough to say no. But maybe I can turn that detail to my advantage by planting a little evidence in his apartment?" Raoul let out a hideous laugh. "Wouldn't that just be a perfect twist to the perfect crime?"

She couldn't believe turning this man down had sent him over the edge. Realizing how close she'd come to actually dating him made her feel ill.

He roughly yanked her from the car until she landed with a hard thud on the musty-smelling blanket.

She closed her eyes against the shaft of pain. For a moment her leg jerked and she hoped the effects of the drug were beginning to wear off. But then Raoul gathered the corners of the blanket together and lifted her up off the ground.

Raoul wasn't a big man, but he was much stronger than he looked. She counted off seconds in her head, trying to estimate how much time passed as she bumped along, before he suddenly dropped her to the ground.

Swamped by a sudden, overwhelming pain, blackness swirled in her mind. It would be so easy to give in to the darkness, but she struggled to remain conscious.

She couldn't let Raoul win.

She refused to give up without a fight!

Finally, he roughly pulled the blanket away from her face, and fresh air filled her nostrils. For several seconds, she reveled in the clean scent. She tried to lift her arms and her legs, and was rewarded by a small flicker of movement.

Close. She was so close to being able to escape. Especially since she didn't see any sign of the drug-soaked rag. Had he left it behind in the car? If so, she needed to take advantage of his mistake.

He was proud of what he'd done. He'd done nothing but talk to her since he'd captured her. She needed to keep him talking. But how?

"Ah, I see you're starting to come around, aren't you, Megan?" Raoul took his time, straightening the corners of the blanket until she was lying in the center of the coarse fabric. "That's so nice. Too bad the clouds are blocking out most of the sun."

He leaned over her, peering down into her face. "You see, I like to look deep into my victims' eyes as I kill them," he whispered.

She wanted to look away but was captivated by the

evil lingering in his eyes. She shivered, knowing he was telling the truth. He enjoyed killing. He was good enough to hide the evidence of his crimes.

And after she was gone, he'd move to Seattle and begin another killing spree all over again.

She couldn't let that happen. Desperately, she tried to flex her muscles, willing her strength to return.

"Don't move," Raoul said, lightly stroking his hand down her bare arm. "I'll be right back."

He was leaving! Thrilled at the opportunity, she gathered every ounce of willpower and strained to move. One inch, and then another. Maybe if she could make it to the edge of the woods, she could hide long enough for someone to notice she was gone and to come after her.

Even though she knew her chances of being rescued were slim to none, she didn't give up. Inch by agonizing inch, she crawled to the edge of the blanket. She felt the softness of grass beneath her fingers when Raoul abruptly returned.

"Tsk, tsk," he muttered, and she heard a soft thud as he dropped whatever he'd been carrying. "You're obviously stronger than I anticipated."

No! She silently screamed in protest when he simply reached down and pressed the sickening-sweet cloth against her face once again.

Helplessly, she stared up at him as the strength in her muscles slowly evaporated.

He'd won. She hadn't been strong enough to get away.

After a minute or two, he tossed the drug-soaked cloth aside and then pulled her back to the center of the blanket. "You see, I need you here on the blanket so there's no chance of stray evidence getting away from me," he said in an oddly matter-of-fact tone.

He pulled on a pair of plastic gloves and then grabbed the brand-new orange polyurethane rope. When he reached down to lift her head, sliding the rope behind her neck, she knew she'd lost.

But a strange sense of peace washed over her. Maybe she was going to die, but she wasn't alone.

The pastor's sermon from the book of Psalms echoed in her mind. *The Lord is my light and my salvation— whom shall I fear? The Lord is the stronghold of my life—of whom should I be afraid?*

Raoul drew the ends of the bright orange rope together until they tightened painfully around her neck. He peered down into her eyes, and instinctively she knew he wanted to see fear reflected in her gaze.

Except she wasn't afraid.

"You're going to die, Megan," he whispered, pulling the rope tighter, cutting off her oxygen. She maintained a serene expression, despite the pain.

"Stop! Leave her alone!"

The shout startled Raoul into dropping the rope. He swung around in shock. From her position on the blanket she caught a glimpse of Sam's tall, lean figure running toward her.

Sam had followed her!

Her wild relief quickly turned to fear when Raoul pulled a gun from the small of his back and took aim.

No! Go back! He has a gun! Go back!

But she couldn't force the words past her bruised and paralyzed throat. Even as she watched, Sam switched directions, heading for the protection of the trees.

Too late. Raoul pulled the trigger and the sound of a gunshot echoed through the night.

To her horror, she saw Sam crumple and fall to the ground.

SIXTEEN

Megan desperately tried to crawl away from Raoul, but her muscles wouldn't cooperate. She managed to move a few inches, but he easily caught her.

"Now you've done it!" Raoul's eyes blazed with fury. "This wasn't part of the plan!"

Please Lord, save Sam. Please spare his life!

She flexed her fingers in the blanket, willing her muscles to obey. Her strength seemed to be returning more quickly this time, and she could only surmise some of the drug in the cloth had already evaporated.

Hoping and praying Sam wasn't fatally wounded and that help was on the way, she stared up at Raoul.

"Won't work," she whispered hoarsely.

"Oh, yes, it will." Raoul didn't seem to be fazed by her returning strength. He gathered the ends of the rope, his gaze fanatical. "You think you'll be strong, but you won't. Eventually, you'll panic." The evil was clear in his eyes when he leaned closer to murmur, "They all do."

She wouldn't, and when he began to pull the ends of the rope tighter, she gathered what was left of her strength and lunged. Using her fingers, she desperately clawed at his face, his eyes.

Raoul reared back, howling in pain. Without wasting a second, she crawled away, putting as much distance between them as possible.

But he wasn't hurt badly enough, and when his hands clamped around her ankles, yanking hard to bring her back, she knew there was no chance for escape.

He swore viciously, grabbed the rope and tied it around her neck. Instantly, red dots swam in her mind and she knew she had less than a minute left.

Bring me home, Lord.

Luke pulled up next to his police-issued vehicle parked conspicuously at the side of the road, and peered through the darkness, his heart thundering in his chest.

Sam had taken his car, calling Luke to let him know how some guy grabbed Megan and was headed toward the old abandoned barn. He could see the barn, but no people.

Where were they?

And then suddenly he saw them. Several yards away. A man, sitting on top of a woman, strangling her with a bright orange rope that seemed to glow in the dark.

Please, Lord, don't let me be too late!

Moving silently, he crept closer. When he was within range, he lifted his weapon and fired. Instantly, the man arched his back in pain, and after several heartbeats, toppled over.

Thank God! Rushing over, he yanked the guy off Megan, taking a moment to verify he was indeed dead. Turning his attention to Megan, he gently brushed her hair away from her eyes. "Megan?"

No response. She didn't even move. Panicked, he

reached down and felt along her neck for a pulse, putting another hand on her chest to check for signs of breathing.

And nearly wept when he felt the irregular beat of Megan's heart beneath his fingertips.

Her eyelids fluttered open and she stared up at him. When she struggled to speak, he shook his head. "Shh, it's okay," he murmured. "You're safe. He's dead. It's over."

She shook her head, urgently. "Sam," she croaked. "Hurt."

Sam? Belatedly remembering his son, Luke jumped up from the blanket and glanced around wildly. "Sam? Where are you?"

"Here." The reply was weak, muffled.

In the darkness he could just make out a figure lying in the grass about halfway between the line of trees and the blanket. Instantly he rushed over. "Are you hurt? What happened?"

"Shot in the leg," Sam murmured, rolling over onto his back and fingering the wound in his right upper thigh. "Tried to get to Megan."

Luke was humbled to realize that Sam had been using his elbows and his uninjured knee to crawl across the ground to help Megan.

They were both alive. Injured but alive!

Thank You, Lord. Thank You!

He quickly called for backup and an ambulance before reaching down to help Sam to his feet.

"Is she okay?" Sam whispered as Luke supported his weight, half carrying him over to Megan.

"She'll be fine." At least he hoped so.

Sam dropped down on the blanket beside Megan, and she reached out to lightly grasp his arm.

"Thanks," she croaked.

"I'm sorry I couldn't stop him," Sam said in a low voice.

She shook her head and smiled. "You did."

When Luke heard Megan's harsh breathing, he grew concerned. "Don't talk," he admonished her. "I'm worried about your throat."

Sirens filled the air, and Luke couldn't help feeling a surge of relief. In the darkness he couldn't see much of Sam's wound, although he did notice his son had tied his shirt around his upper thigh to help stop the bleeding. Pride surged in his chest.

When the paramedics arrived, Luke waved them over. Within moments the two people he loved most in the world, Megan and Sam, were bundled up on stretchers.

When the paramedics tried to lift Megan into the ambulance, she shook her head and reached out to grasp his arm. "Blanket," she whispered.

"What?" Luke didn't understand. He glanced over his shoulder at the blanket lying on the ground. What about the blanket?

"Evidence. Other murders." The urgency in her voice, the alarmed expression in her eyes, finally helped him to understand.

"Are you saying he used this blanket for other victims?" he asked in a low voice.

She nodded vigorously, finally relaxing her grip from his arm.

"Okay, I understand. I'll take care of it." He stepped back so the paramedics could slide the gurney inside.

His deputies had arrived with the ambulance. He walked over to Frank and handed him his gun. "Here, you're going to want to test this to match the ballistics with the slug in our suspect. And I want you to carefully wrap up the blanket and send it to the crime lab to be tested for evidence," he ordered.

"Where are you going?" Frank demanded.

"I killed a man tonight, which means I'm required to step down from my duties until there's been an investigation." Luke didn't hesitate to use the rules in his favor. And after his conversation with the mayor earlier, officially he wasn't the interim sheriff anymore.

Besides, none of that mattered right now. He couldn't bear to be away from Sam and Megan for a moment longer. "I'll be at Hope County Hospital if you need me."

"But—"

Luke ignored Frank's sputtering as he turned and walked away.

At the hospital, Luke discovered Sam had already been taken into surgery. The swift action of the hospital staff made him realize his son might have been injured worse than he thought. He closed his eyes and prayed.

Please Lord, keep Sam safe in Your care.

When he asked about Megan, he was relieved she was still being seen in the emergency department. When they tried to give him some song and dance about only allowing family to visit, he flashed his badge and bullied his way in to see her.

"How are you doing?" He crossed over to her bedside, taking her hand in his.

She smiled but couldn't nod her head, even though

she tried, because of the huge ice pack covering her throat.

"Don't talk," he murmured, pulling up a chair next to her. For a moment all he could do was to clutch her hand, resting his forehead on her arm, drawing from her strength to help hold himself together.

So close. Too close. If he'd been a few seconds later, he would have lost her. And Sam, too. There was no doubt in his mind that the killer would have gone after Sam to silence him forever.

Thank God he'd left the mayor standing there and had taken off after Sam the moment his son had called to let him know about Megan.

Those moments would be forever engraved in his memory.

Only once before had he been forced to draw his gun and shoot a suspect, and that was during his first two years on the force.

He hadn't intended to kill the man, but only to get him off Megan.

Unfortunately, his aim had been a little too good.

Forgive me, Lord.

Megan tugged at her hand and he pulled his scattered thoughts together, glancing down at her questioningly. She made writing motions with her hand.

There was a clipboard with paper and a pencil on the bedside table. He handed it over to her and she wrote only one word.

Sam?

He tried not to let his fear show. "They'd already taken him to surgery by the time I got here. Hopefully we'll hear something soon."

She frowned and then picked up the pencil again. *I'm sorry.*

"Don't, Megan. None of this is your fault. Sam will be fine. He might have lost a little blood, but I'm sure he'll recover quickly enough."

Her gaze was skeptical, as if she didn't quite believe him. Then she picked up the pencil again and began to write. *Raoul confessed to killing many women. Sherman didn't kill anyone other than Katie. It was all Raoul.*

"Raoul?" The use of the guy's first name floored him. "You actually know this guy?"

"He worked in the Chicago crime lab," she whispered.

"Don't talk, write," he said. He remembered her talking about Raoul Lee, but hadn't realized he was the same guy who'd just tried to kill her. But now her theory made total sense. "I guess you were right, Megan. The killer was someone who worked in the system."

Personal. He was upset with me, so he made this personal.

He looked at the note she'd written and nodded. "You're safe now, though. No one else will suffer at his hands."

The Lord was watching over us. She'd underscored the sentiment twice for added emphasis.

He couldn't help but smile. He was thrilled she'd found faith. And he totally agreed with her.

The Lord had watched over them tonight. "I was so worried about you, Megan," he confessed in a low voice. "When Sam called me I nearly lost my mind."

She stared at him, searching his gaze with hers. He could tell there was something she wanted to say, but she didn't write anything down. She didn't have to, because he understood her unspoken question.

"I'm sorry if you thought I didn't care about you," he said slowly. "When Sam accused me of letting my feelings for you get in the way of the investigation, I thought maybe he was right. That if I'd only been working harder, I could have prevented what happened to Amy. Especially after hearing her parents all but accuse him of murdering their daughter."

His shame and guilt hadn't just been about how he'd handled the investigation, he realized now, but the fact that Sam had been upset to find Megan in his arms. Sam hadn't come to grips with the idea of his father seeing a woman.

Luke now knew how much he loved her. With his entire heart and soul. But no matter how much he loved Megan, he couldn't risk doing anything that might harm his relationship with his son.

There was simply no easy way to explain.

"I care about you, Megan. More than you'll ever know. But Sam—well, he still needs me. And right now, I need to stay focused on Sam."

When she frowned a little, he realized he needed to be blunt.

"I care about you, but I can't spare time for a relationship. I'm sorry." When he glanced at her, his heart squeezed when he saw her eyes were bright with unshed tears.

She blinked them away and picked up her clipboard. *I understand. Just know I care about you, too.*

"Ms. O'Ryan?" The nurse poked her head into the room. "The doctor has decided to admit you for observation overnight. Edie and I are going to move you upstairs."

Megan tried to nod.

"You can come, too," the nurse said kindly.

Luke shook his head. "I'm waiting for my son to get out of surgery." He stepped back as the nurse took the clipboard away from Megan and set it on the bedside table. The nursing assistant, Edie, unlocked the brakes on the bed.

As they wheeled Megan away, she lifted a hand to wave goodbye.

He had to force himself to stay where he was and not follow her. His gaze landed on the clipboard they'd left behind.

In the center of the page, in Megan's handwriting, was one last message.

I love you.

Megan spooned another ice chip into her mouth, closing her eyes as the coldness soothed her sore throat.

Swallowing and talking didn't hurt as much today as it had last night. Apparently the anti-inflammatory medications were starting to work.

But all morning she'd been waiting for the doctor to show up. The nurses kept reassuring her he'd be here soon.

Not soon enough for her, though.

Finally there was a brief knock on her door. Before she could even respond, it swung open.

"Good afternoon!" Dr. DePaul greeted her jovially. She had to admit, she'd never been in a hospital where the employees were as cheerful as they were here at

Hope County Hospital. "How are you feeling, young lady?"

Not like a young lady, that's for sure. But since Dr. DePaul looked old enough to be her grandfather, she didn't take offense. "Better." Too bad her voice still sounded like a bullfrog.

A sick bullfrog.

"Excellent. Now open your mouth for me," he instructed, pulling out his penlight. She obediently opened her mouth and he peered down inside her throat. "The swelling looks a little better, but I think you're going to have to take it easy for a couple of days."

She moved the ice bag so she could nod. "Home?" she asked.

"Yes, I think we can discharge you today, but not until later this evening. I'd like you to get one more intravenous dose of your anti-inflammatory medication first, and it's not due until six o'clock tonight."

She wasn't about to argue, since she would have to figure out how she was going to get a ride anyway. And she wasn't going home, but back to the motel. Luke had stopped in briefly earlier that morning to tell her that Sam was recovering fine from surgery, but he hadn't stayed long.

Had he seen her note? Maybe not.

Did it really matter? He'd made his position clear. Even if he cared about her, he wasn't going to pursue anything further between them.

And as much as the mere thought made her heart break, she understood. Luke wouldn't sacrifice his relationship with Sam.

She wouldn't ask him to.

Leaning back against the pillows, she racked her

brain trying to think of who else she could call for a ride. Josie? Frank?

She was ashamed to realize she hadn't made many friends here in Crystal Lake.

A situation she needed to fix, as soon as possible. Because even though Raoul was dead, she'd decided she wasn't going back to Chicago.

She was going to take Bryan up on his offer of a full-time position. If the offer was still open. It was possible that after he discovered the truth about Raoul, he wouldn't be so eager to allow her to stay on.

And if he didn't, then she'd keep doing her part-time work until the DNA lab was caught up. Maybe something else would open up then.

She wanted to stay, not just because of Luke and Sam, but because of the community. The church.

She finally felt as if she'd come home. She needed a new place to stay of course, but Crystal Lake was going to be her home.

She must have dozed, because a soft knock at her door startled her. "Come in," she croaked.

The door swung open and Sam stood uncertainly on the threshold, balancing precariously on crutches. "Hey," he said awkwardly. "Can I come in?"

Stunned, she could only nod.

Laboriously, he made his way over to her bedside, leaning heavily on the crutches, tiny rivulets of sweat sliding down the sides of his face.

"Are you supposed to be up?" she asked doubtfully.

"Yes, I have to walk fifty feet if I want to go home. But I can't stay long," he added sheepishly. "Dad went down to the cafeteria for something to eat and I have to get back before he returns."

She wasn't sure she understood Sam's reasoning, but she didn't argue. "I hope the surgery wasn't too bad," she whispered.

"I'm fine. You're the one I was worried about." Sam hung his head for a moment. "I'm sorry I couldn't get to you sooner. You probably wouldn't have ended up here in the hospital if I had."

"Sam!" She said his name as loud as she could, which wasn't very loud at all. "You saved my life. He shot you because of me. I'm forever in your debt."

"I wasn't very nice to you," he said in a low tone. "And I came here to ask you to give my dad another chance."

She stared in shock. "What do you mean?"

"I've been trying to convince him that you're the best thing that's happened to him, but he won't listen. I figured it was because you pushed him away. Because of me. Because of the way I acted toward you."

"Oh, Sam," she murmured, trying to think of a way to explain that she hadn't been the one to push Luke away without adding to Sam's guilt.

"I went a little crazy after Amy died," Sam confessed. "And it made me realize how much my dad went through after my mom died. I didn't give him enough credit. I was awful to him."

"Sam, your father loves you. Never forget that, not for a minute," she said.

"I don't want him to lose you, too," Sam continued, as if he hadn't heard what she'd said. "So can't you give him another chance? Please?"

She glanced over Sam's shoulder to see Luke standing in the doorway, his expression full of hopeful amazement. Without breaking eye contact with Luke, she nodded, "Yes, of course I'll give him another chance. As many chances as he needs."

"Sam? Did you really mean all that?" Luke asked, venturing further into the room.

Sam swung around to face his father, his face growing a little red as he realized his father had overheard everything. But then he lifted his chin. "Yes, I do. Megan is great, and I don't want you to blow it."

Luke wrapped his arm around Sam's shoulders, giving Megan a broad grin. "Well, okay, then." Luke came over to the other side of the bed to take her hand. "Megan, I know you only came to Crystal Lake to heal after your sister's death."

"I love it here," Megan said quickly. She felt a tiny pang in her heart when she thought of Katie.

But she also knew that her sister was in a much better place now.

Luke had showed her that.

"You do?" Luke sounded a bit surprised. Then he cleared his throat loudly. "Megan, will you do me the honor of being my wife?"

"Wife?" she squeaked in surprise. She hadn't expected a proposal!

She glanced at Sam, not sure this was what he'd intended when he'd asked her to give Luke another chance. But the expectant smile on his face convinced her otherwise.

Her heart swelled with love and joy.

How could she say no?

"Yes, Luke. I'd love to be your wife." She couldn't think of anything better than staying in Crystal Lake with Sam and Luke.

Home at last.

EPILOGUE

Dressed in the traditional white gown, Megan waited in the back of the church as the music changed to the wedding march.

Slowly, everyone in the small congregation rose to their feet and turned to face her.

Not feeling the least bit nervous, she walked down the aisle holding on to Frank's arm. Josie, the owner of Rose's Café, stood up at the altar as her matron of honor, and Sam stood beside his father as the best man, so handsome in his tux she wanted to cry.

Luke watched her approach, a proud smile on his face. She couldn't hold back her own smile, either. Last month the people of Crystal Lake had officially voted him in as sheriff.

Luke, Sam and Megan weren't outsiders in Crystal Lake anymore. They belonged to the town.

And the town belonged to them, too.

The crowded church was a silent testament to that fact.

At the front of the church, she kissed Frank on the cheek and then put her hand in Luke's. Together, they stood before the pastor.

"Dearly beloved, we gather here today to witness

the holy marriage of Lucas Francis Torretti and Megan Katherine O'Ryan."

Francis? Luke's middle name was Francis? She glanced up at him, trying to swallow a giggle.

The wry twist to his mouth and the tightening of his hand on hers helped her to keep it together. Barely.

But the private joke kept a smile on her face throughout the rest of the ceremony.

And when Luke bent toward her to kiss her, her heart swelled with love.

"I love you, Luke Francis Torretti," she whispered.

"Mrs. Megan Torretti, I love you too," he whispered back.

And she knew, when she caught a glimpse of Sam's broad smile as the church attendees applauded, that she was the luckiest woman in the whole world.

* * * * *

Dear Reader,

I've always been fascinated by the forensic work of crime scene investigators. Science was my favorite subject in college, and I'm impressed at how tiny microscopic details can assist in capturing the bad guys. As a result, I decided to make CSI work the focus of my next few stories.

In this book, Megan suffers the tragic loss of her sister, causing her to give up her career as a crime scene investigator. But when Interim Sheriff Lucas Torretti needs help processing the crime scene of an innocent young girl, she can't bring herself to refuse.

Luke is struggling in his relationship with his teenage son, Sam, who appears to be a magnet for trouble. Circumstantial evidence links his son to the crime, and a kernel of doubt forms in the back of his mind. Megan's support helps to keep him focused on the case. But soon, tragedy and danger bring Luke and Sam together, especially after Sam risks his own life to save Megan from a deranged killer.

Faith, love and danger are the themes of *Lawman-in-Charge,* and I hope you enjoy Megan and Luke's story. I'm always thrilled to hear from my readers, and I can be reached through my website at www.laurascottbooks. com.

Yours in faith,
Laura Scott

QUESTIONS FOR DISCUSSION

1. In the beginning of the story, Megan thinks she's going crazy after she imagines she hears her dead sister calling her name. Have you ever felt this way? Why or why not?

2. Early in the story Megan and Luke both feel as if they are outsiders in the small town of Crystal Lake. Has there been a time you felt like an outsider, and how did you overcome that feeling?

3. Luke struggled very hard to overcome the loss of his wife and nearly losing his son. He renewed his faith to get his life back on track. Has there been a time when your faith has helped you to get over a horrible mistake that you'd made? If so, how?

4. Luke quickly becomes Megan's protector even though he'd rather keep his distance on a personal level. How does his turbulent relationship with his son influence his growing relationship with Megan?

5. Megan has to cope with her guilt over her sister's death. Has there been a time when you've had to cope with guilt? Please discuss.

6. At one point in the story, Luke begins to fear his son Sam might be involved in the murder he's investigating. His instinct is to protect his son over doing his job. Did you agree with his actions? Why or why not?

7. Megan finds herself in the back of the small-town church with Luke by her side. Discuss this scene and how it became the turning point emotionally for Megan.

8. Megan begins to pray when she's run off the road by the murderer. Describe a time when you realized the power of prayer.

9. Luke's son, Sam, accuses him of letting his relationship with Megan distract him from finding his girlfriend's murderer. Luke pushes Megan away, because deep down he feels his son might have been right. Has there been a time when you pushed a loved one away, instead of leaning on them for support? Discuss.

10. When Megan is captured by the murderer, Sam risks his life to save her. Have you ever had to put your safety on the line for someone else? And if not, how do you think you would handle a similar situation? Why?

11. At what point in the story does Megan fully support her faith in God? Discuss if you've ever had a similar experience.

12. How does Luke convince Megan of the true depth of his love? How did his faith impact this realization?

INSPIRATIONAL

Inspirational romances to warm your heart & soul

TITLES AVAILABLE NEXT MONTH

Available July 12, 2011

THE INNOCENT WITNESS
Protection Specialists
Terri Reed

HER GUARDIAN
Sharon Dunn

DEAD RECKONING
Rachelle McCalla

DANGEROUS REUNION
Sandra Robbins

LISCNM0611

REQUEST YOUR FREE BOOKS!

2 FREE RIVETING INSPIRATIONAL NOVELS
PLUS 2 FREE MYSTERY GIFTS

Love Inspired®
SUSPENSE

YES! Please send me 2 FREE Love Inspired® Suspense novels and my 2 FREE mystery gifts (gifts are worth about $10). After receiving them, if I don't wish to receive any more books, I can return the shipping statement marked "cancel". If I don't cancel, I will receive 4 brand-new novels every month and be billed just $4.24 per book in the U.S. or $4.74 per book in Canada. That's a saving of at least 23% off the cover price. It's quite a bargain! Shipping and handling is just 50¢ per book in the U.S. and 75¢ per book in Canada.* I understand that accepting the 2 free books and gifts places me under no obligation to buy anything. I can always return a shipment and cancel at any time. Even if I never buy another book, the two free books and gifts are mine to keep forever.

123/323 IDN FDCT

Name	(PLEASE PRINT)	

Address		Apt. #

City	State/Prov.	Zip/Postal Code

Signature (if under 18, a parent or guardian must sign)

Mail to the **Reader Service:**
IN U.S.A.: P.O. Box 1867, Buffalo, NY 14240-1867
IN CANADA: P.O. Box 609, Fort Erie, Ontario L2A 5X3

Not valid for current subscribers to Love Inspired Suspense books.

**Are you a subscriber to Love Inspired Suspense
and want to receive the larger-print edition?
Call 1-800-873-8635 or visit www.ReaderService.com.**

* Terms and prices subject to change without notice. Prices do not include applicable taxes. Sales tax applicable in N.Y. Canadian residents will be charged applicable taxes. Offer not valid in Quebec. This offer is limited to one order per household. All orders subject to credit approval. Credit or debit balances in a customer's account(s) may be offset by any other outstanding balance owed by or to the customer. Please allow 4 to 6 weeks for delivery. Offer available while quantities last.

Your Privacy—The Reader Service is committed to protecting your privacy. Our Privacy Policy is available online at www.ReaderService.com or upon request from the Reader Service.

We make a portion of our mailing list available to reputable third parties that offer products we believe may interest you. If you prefer that we not exchange your name with third parties, or if you wish to clarify or modify your communication preferences, please visit us at www.ReaderService.com/consumerschoice or write to us at Reader Service Preference Service, P.O. Box 9062, Buffalo, NY 14269. Include your complete name and address.

LISUS11

Love Inspired

After losing his wife and son, Adrian Lapp has vowed never to marry again. But widow Faith Martin—the newest resident of the Amish community of Hope Springs—captivates him from their first meeting. Can Adrian open his heart to the possibility of love again?

The Farmer Next Door
by Patricia Davids

BRIDES OF
Amish Country

*Available in July
wherever books are sold.*

www.LoveInspiredBooks.com

LI87679

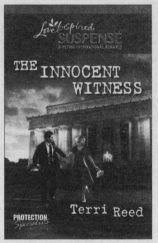